Praise for
RODMAN PHILBRICK'S
REM World

"Non-stop action and adventure abound in this otherworld fantasy."
— *Childhood Education*

"Imaginative characters and a string of cliffhangers make Philbrick's
science-fiction novel a fun and fast-paced read .... These vivid person-
alities will usher readers quickly through the chapters."
— *Publishers Weekly*

"A fast and furious journey into an alternative universe .... Young Harry
Potter fans ... will recognize the misfit hero in a strange, new world."
— *Booklist*

"Philbrick's narrative voice is exciting and pulls the right strings."
— *School Library Journal*

Other Signature Titles

Freak the Mighty
Rodman Philbrick

The Fire Pony
Rodman Philbrick

Afternoon of the Elves
Janet Taylor Lisle

Somewhere in the Darkness
Walter Dean Myers

The Classroom at the End of the Hall
Douglas Evans

Bad Girls
Cynthia Voigt

REM World

World

Rodman Philbrick

SCHOLASTIC SIGNATURE

AN IMPRINT OF SCHOLASTIC INC.

NEW YORK TORONTO LONDON AUCKLAND SYDNEY
MEXICO CITY NEW DELHI HONG KONG BUENOS AIRES

No part of this publication may be reproduced in whole or in part, or stored in a retrieval system, or transmitted in any form or by any means, electronic, mechanical, photocopying, recording, or otherwise, without written permission of the publisher. For information regarding permission, write to Scholastic Inc., Attention: Permissions Department, 557 Broadway, New York, NY 10012.

This book was originally published in hardcover by the Blue Sky Press in 2000.

ISBN 0-439-08363-X

12 11 10 9 8 7 6 5 4   4 5 6 7/0

Printed in the U.S.A.   40

First Scholastic trade paperback printing, March 2002

Designed by Jennifer Rinaldi

FOR PATRICK DELLASANTA,

WHOSE SECRET NAME IS COURAGE

CONTENTS

· · ·

1

■ ■ ■

FAT
NO MORE

ARTHUR WOODBURY WAS fat, quite fat, and the nickname he hated most of all, the one that made his ears hot, was Biscuit Butt. He hated being Biscuit Butt more than he hated being Arty Farty, or Jelly Belly, or Fat Boy, or even the dreaded Goodyear. Mean but true, because as everybody knew, Goodyear was a blimp.

And so on his eleventh birthday (yes, he ate the whole cake), the human blimp named Arthur Woodbury made a decision that would change not only his life but the fate of the whole world, and ultimately the entire universe, and many other universes, too.

Arthur decided he would be fat no more. Somehow he would get thin. Gloriously, triumphantly thin. So thin, he would amaze his friends.

Except that, strictly speaking, he had no friends. Not even one. The only friends he had were the kind you ate, like sugarcoated cupcakes or nut-filled candy bars or double-scoop chocolate-chip ice-cream cones.

Arthur lived with his mother, and his mother lived with her mother, and so the three of them lived together in the kind of stupefying silence that was only broken by the creak of the refrigerator door.

Creak, a cold pork chop.

Creak, that plate of barbecued chicken wings.

Creak, more biscuits.

It had to stop, Arthur decided. And the truly wonderful thing, the fantastically amazing thing, was this: He didn't have to stop eating. He didn't have to go on a diet. He didn't have to exercise.

All he had to do was sleep.

LOSE WEIGHT WHILE YOU SLEEP!
TRY THE MIRACULOUS
REM SLEEP DEVICE.
SATISFACTION GUARANTEED.
SEND ONLY $9.99 TO
REM WORLD PRODUCTS.

That's what the ad promised on the back page

of the comic book. For a mere nine dollars and ninety-nine cents, Arthur could go to sleep fat and wake up thin.

He'd sent for it weeks and weeks ago and had pretty much given up hope—rooked again by those cheesy comic books—when the package arrived exactly on his eleventh birthday.

"Oh," his mother had said, sounding just a little surprised. "Someone sent you a birthday present—isn't that nice?"

Arthur agreed that it was very nice indeed. He neglected to mention that he had sent himself the present, because sometimes the less mothers know, the better.

Not that Arthur's mom was a bad mother. Exactly the reverse was true. She was as good as a mother could be, considering that Arthur's dad had died before he was born, and he'd had no father to teach him important stuff like baseball and night crawlers and how to pick your nose without getting caught.

Arthur's mom tried hard, but sometimes she had no idea what her son was thinking, or why the only thing that made him happy was food, more food. Endless supplies of food, glorious food.

"Did you have a nice birthday, dear?" she asked. "Was the cake big enough?"

But Arthur didn't answer because he wasn't listening. He was thinking about his new miracle weight-loss device. If only it would work! If only he really could go to sleep fat and wake up thin!

On the way out of the kitchen, Arthur snagged eleven Oreo cookies and slipped them into his over-sized pockets. Just for luck. Then he headed down the cellar stairs into the deep, dark basement.

And his life, and the world, and the universe would never be the same again.

2

...

UNDER THE
BIG BAD WORLD

FOR SOME REASON the basement always reminded
Arthur of his late father. Not that he had ever known
him, outside of photographs and that stupid wedding
video his mother liked to watch sometimes late at
night. But there was a workbench in the basement,
and racks of tools, and the stuff certainly didn't
belong to Mom or Gramma, neither of whom could
turn a screwdriver without falling down. So the tools
had been his father's, once upon a time, and Arthur
supposed that someday they would be his. Saws and
hammers and pry-bars and sharp-edged things that
would cut off his fingers if he wasn't careful.

Other boys learned about tools from their dads,

who also took them to Cub Scouts and soccer and other boy-dad things. And when the dads were hanging out by themselves, talking dads-only stuff, the boys would brag about their fathers. How they'd almost been big-league ballplayers, and how they were strong enough to lift a whole pickup truck if they felt like it, and all the medals they'd won in the war. Each boy trying to prove that his dad was the biggest, the smartest, the fastest, the strongest, the best dad in the whole world.

Arthur didn't have anything to brag about because his father was dead, and if he happened to mention that, well, all the bragging stopped, and it got real quiet. And then, inevitably, one of the other boys would smirk and break the uncomfortable silence by saying, "Arty Farty had a father? I don't think so. His mother bought him at the bakery. That's why he's got a GREAT BIG BISCUIT BUTT!"

Which sometimes made Arthur think his father must have been a loser. What kind of dad died before his son was born? A loser dad, that's what kind. One who didn't care enough to stay alive. Arthur knew it wasn't fair to blame his dad for being dead, but he couldn't help it. Being called Biscuit Butt made him feel unreasonable. Like he'd been cheated out of something really important before he even knew what it was.

Now, going down into the basement on the afternoon of his eleventh birthday, Arthur was thinking how cool it would be if his dad suddenly just appeared out of nowhere. "Sorry, kid, I'm not your late father, I'm just late."

Like he'd never actually died and the whole thing was just a misunderstanding.

What a lame idea. It was such a stupid idea, it made Arthur hungry, and he reached into his pocket to snag one of the Oreo cookies.

Mmmm. He could almost taste the velvety chocolate dissolving on his tongue, and the way the sweet vanilla filling made his whole mouth go *zing*!

Then, for reasons he didn't quite understand—a mysterious feeling that came from deep inside—he decided that just for once he'd put off eating the Oreo and save it for later.

Which was a good thing, as it turned out, because before long, the cookie would save his life.

SATISFACTION GUARANTEED.

That was the phrase that really hooked Arthur when he first saw the advertisement for the REM Sleep Device—even though he knew from long experience that satisfaction can't be guaranteed, not even if you get an extra dessert.

He couldn't tell what the actual device was from the picture, which was sort of blurry, and Arthur had been prepared for the worst. Probably the thing would be made out of cheap plastic, like those toys they gave away at fast-food restaurants. How cool could it be for only nine dollars and ninety-nine cents? His mom had spent more than that on his birthday cake, what with all the extra frosting.

So when Arthur opened up the smooth box marked REM WORLD PRODUCTS, he was pleasantly surprised. Very pleasantly surprised. Because inside, glowing like the darkest part of a cat's eye, was a shiny black device that certainly wasn't made of cheap plastic. Hard to say what it was made of, except that it was cool to the touch, and it seemed to shimmer slightly as Arthur carefully lifted it out of the trim little container.

Before Arthur had a chance to read the instructions, the mysterious-looking device opened on its own. As if triggered by a hidden spring, it suddenly unfolded and seemed to grow right before his startled eyes.

In less than the time it took for his heart to beat twice, the REM Sleep Device became a special helmet, with a black-tinted visor that slipped down to cover the eyes.

"Wow," said Arthur, and he meant it.

The instructions were printed on a single sheet of very thin paper.

Congratulations! You are now the proud owner of a REM Sleep Device. Batteries are not included because batteries are not required. The REM Sleep Device works on brainpower. It will help you harness the hidden power of the human mind. With the aid of the REM Sleep Device you'll not only lose unwanted pounds while you sleep, you'll increase your powers of imagination and therefore become more intelligent. You'll awaken thinner and smarter, although not necessarily wiser.

All you have to do is follow these simple rules:

1. Put on the REM Sleep Device.

2. Lie down in a safe place.

3. Go to sleep.

WARNING!

All rules must be followed exactly,

or the REM World Products guarantee will be void.

These are the easiest instructions I ever read, Arthur said to himself.

He couldn't wait to try it.

There were no beds in the basement, so Arthur hopped on the workbench. He put down the sheet of instructions and picked up the glistening black helmet. He knew even before he tried it on that the device would fit perfectly, and it did.

"This is so cool," Arthur said as the visor automatically flipped down to cover his eyes.

Inside the helmet he could hear a faint, distant sound, like waves breaking on a faraway beach. It was like the sound you hear when you hold a shell to your ear, only more so: *Sssssssssh, sssssssssssh, sssssssssssssh*, the sleepy whisper of an enchanted wind.

Arthur lay down on the workbench. He didn't even have to close his eyes, because the visor made everything totally dark. The sound of the distant ocean came closer, closer.

Sssssssssssh, the wind whispered. *Sssssssssssssssssssssh*.

And then, just like that, Arthur fell deeply asleep.

3

. . .

LOW TIDE
IN REM WORLD

W HEN A RTHUR WOKE UP he was still fat. That was
the first thing he checked, even before he took the
helmet off and sat up.

"I knew it," he said bitterly. "What a rip-off! The
stupid thing doesn't work."

And with that, he threw the REM Sleep Device to
the basement floor. It skittered away into a dark corner, sounding almost as if it were alive instead of just
a stupid old helmet bought from the back pages of a
comic book.

The second thing he noticed was that the seashell
sound of the ocean was still there, even though he
was no longer wearing the helmet.

"Weird," said Arthur, climbing down off the workbench. Maybe it was just wind in the trees. But no, he knew what wind-in-the-trees sounded like, and this was different.

Maybe it was an approaching tornado, or a hurricane.

"Cool!" said Arthur, who enjoyed a storm so long as he was safe in the basement, or huddled under his bed with a flashlight and plenty of candy bars.

Cautiously he went to the bulkhead and unlatched the old wooden door. The ocean-roar sound got much louder. Except it couldn't be the ocean, because the seashore was miles and miles away.

What was going on out there in the big bad world?

Curiosity got the best of Arthur, and so he went up the bulkhead steps to lift the door. Arthur decided the noise must be some sort of machinery, maybe a huge leaf blower, coming from the yard next door.

They'd better not blow all their crummy old leaves my way, Arthur said to himself, and he flung open the bulkhead door and climbed up out of the basement and into his own backyard.

Except it wasn't his own backyard.

Arthur was standing on the hard, shiny mud of a beach at low tide. Clumps of green seaweed had been left behind by the retreating sea. All along the horizon, in the direction of where the ocean must have gone, was a thick white mist.

And the sky was not blue. It was pale green.

· · ·

Impossible. Arthur decided the best thing to do was to go back into the basement and start over. But when he looked behind him, the bulkhead door had vanished, and there was nothing there but the same hard, damp mud and a few more globs of fragrant seaweed.

"I love that smell," said a small voice.

"What!" said Arthur as his heart thumped. He looked wildly around for the source of the small voice, but he couldn't see anything.

"Over here," the voice said.

Arthur whirled around, but he still couldn't see anything, or anyone.

"I'm right here, kid. If you got any closer I'd bite— except, lucky for you, I don't bite."

At last Arthur was able to make out the source of the voice. Behind him a small, plump creature sat on a lump of seaweed. You had to look close because it blended into the background, as if camouflaged. Arthur squinted and saw that it looked like an opossum, because of the long, curvy tail, but it also resembled a cat with very large, dark brown eyes.

"What *are* you?" Arthur exclaimed.

The creature looked offended. "I'm not a *what*. I'm a *who*."

"Sorry," said Arthur, who felt bad. "Do you have a name?"

"Morf." The creature raised a paw to its forehead

and seemed to concentrate, as if trying to dredge up thoughts from the very air. "And your name is, let me see...wait, don't tell me...Biscuit! That's what I'm picking up. You're Mr. Biscuit, right?"

Arthur felt his face go red. "My name is Arthur," he insisted.

"Hmmmm," said Morf. "If you say so."

"I *do* say so."

"Arthur Biscuit?"

"Look, please forget the biscuit part, okay? It's just plain Arthur."

"Anything you say," said Morf. "But around here you have to earn a name before you get to keep it."

With that, Morf got up from the pile of seaweed, raised his slightly muddy paw, and shook the boy's hand.

"Welcome to REM World," he said. "I'll be your guide. Every visitor to REM World gets a guide."

"REM World?" said Arthur. "Guide? What are you talking about?"

"Didn't you read the instructions?"

"Of course I read the instructions," Arthur said indignantly. "And it didn't say anything about my house disappearing. Or finding myself on a beach with all this stinky seaweed and a sky that's green instead of blue."

"Uh-oh!" Morf looked at him with sudden concern. "Where's your helmet?"

"Helmet?"

"I knew it!" Morf said. "If you read *both* sides of the instructions, you'd know you can't leave your helmet behind. Oh, this is bad, very bad! Terrible things will happen! How are you supposed to get home without your helmet?"

Arthur had no idea what Morf was talking about, and no desire to find out. What he wanted to find was a way back into his basement. He searched around for the vanished bulkhead, but it was as if his home had never existed. "This must be a dream," he decided. "That's it! A dream. All I have to do is close my eyes and count to three and I'll wake up. One...two..."

"Sorry, kid, but that trick won't work here."

Arthur opened his eyes and found he was still in REM World, wherever that was. Stupid helmet. If only he'd read the instructions more thoroughly, instead of just skimming. "What am I going to do?"

"I suggest we run," Morf said.

"Run?" asked Arthur. He hated to run. "Why?"

"Because they're coming to get us," said Morf with a shrug, as if he couldn't care less.

"What are you talking about?" asked Arthur.

"Monsters," Morf said, even more casually. "Fog Monsters."

That's when Arthur saw them. Large, murky shapes stumbling through the mist. And they really were monsters.

4

. . .

THINGS IN
THE WHITE MIST

ARTHUR RAN, BUT the hard-packed mud was slippery underfoot and he couldn't seem to get any traction. Truth was, he'd always been the slowest one in gym class, which was just one of the many reasons he hated exercise. But what choice did he have?

Every time he looked over his shoulder, the things in the fog kept getting closer and closer.

"Uh-oh," said Morf, skidding to a stop.

Arthur almost ran over him and ended up— *whump!*—on his bottom in the wet mud.

"What do you mean 'uh-oh'?" he asked fearfully. "Hadn't we better keep running?"

"Too late," said Morf. "We're surrounded."

It was true. The Fog Monsters were coming at them from all directions. Great, lumbering beasts whose shapes seemed to change as they got closer and closer.

Arthur decided the best thing to do was close his eyes and wait for the end. He couldn't run anymore. His butt was soaking wet. The things in the fog were going to get him, and there was nothing he could do about it.

"It won't be long now," Morf said cheerfully, and he began to groom his tail with his small, fussy fingers.

Arthur kept his eyes shut tight. He could hear Morf purring happily away, and he could also hear the gloppy, mud-sucking sound of the Fog Monsters getting closer and closer.

Closer and closer.

Finally he couldn't stand it any longer, and he opened his eyes just a little.

What he saw surprised him so much, he fell over backwards—*sploosh!* "Yow!" he screamed, and he struggled to sit up.

Instead of Fog Monsters, he was surrounded by more than a dozen froglike creatures. They were bigger than he was, but not monster size. They had green, mottled skin, and pale white bellies, and rubbery arms and legs. Their sad-looking eyes seemed to be studying him with great intensity. At once, he knew that they meant him no harm.

"Greetings," the largest one croaked. Its voice was

so deep and wet-sounding, it made Arthur's ears rattle. "Welcome to REM World. I am Galump, mother of the Frog People."

Arthur was so shocked—and so relieved—he couldn't speak.

"He didn't read his instructions," Morf warned. "Forgot his helmet."

"No!"

Morf nodded glumly. "I'm afraid so."

Galump sighed, and it sounded exactly like the lowest note on a tuba. "No one has ever forgotten his helmet before," she said, and her big, sad-looking eyes slowly blinked. "This is a matter of grave concern. Very grave concern. You'd better come along with us. First we'll feed, and then we'll see what kind of trouble you're in."

They all headed off into the mist.

"It wasn't my fault about the helmet," Arthur whispered to Morf. "How was I supposed to know there were two sides to the instructions?"

"There are two sides to everything," Morf pointed out.

Arthur tried to change the subject. "If the Frog People are so nice, why did you call them Fog Monsters?"

Morf shrugged and twitched his tail. "So I made a mistake. Nobody's perfect."

As they marched farther and farther into the mist, Galump saw that Arthur was having trouble keeping up. "I carried my children on my back when they were young," she explained. "There's no reason I can't carry you."

And so it was that a friendless fat boy named Arthur Woodbury found himself being borne like a king by the wise and venerable Galump, ruler of a fabled queendom at the bottom of the sea.

"Cool," said Arthur as his new friends trundled him along, into the white mist, into a world he'd never seen before. "Maybe I like this place after all. Just a little."

"Too bad about the helmet," said Morf, who was riding on Galump's other shoulder.

"Who cares about the stupid helmet!" Arthur retorted. "Why does everybody keep mentioning the helmet? So I forgot it! What's the big deal?"

"Nothing much," said Morf. "You violated one of the laws of the universe, that's all." Morf yawned and patted his paw against his mouth. "Traveling makes me sleepy. Wake me when we get there."

And with that, he curled up and covered his eyes with his tail and slept all the way to Mud City.

. . .

As it turned out, the ancient place called Mud City wasn't made of mud at all, but of a strong, rock-hard substance. The city reminded Arthur of the mud castles he'd made at the beach when he was little. But unlike Arthur's mud castles, these were beautiful and elegant, with mud-dribble towers that soared high above the endless mist, and arching dribble-bridges connecting each building to the next. The whole city was reflected in the hard, shiny mud upon which it was built, and Arthur had never seen anything so enchanting in his whole life.

Everywhere he looked, Arthur saw something new and fascinating about the ingenious way one building seemed to flow into the next without looking crowded or uncomfortable.

There were many fine touches and details. What looked like laurels of seaweed draped over the windows and doorways were actually carved right into the "mud." Many of the walls had been decorated with dribble-pictures of Galump's ancestors, the very first Frog People. It was as if each dribble-building had a story to tell, but instead of words the story was written in shapes. And if you put all the building-stories together, it was a book called *Mud City*, and you read it by living there.

"This is so cool!" Arthur exclaimed. "This has got to be the neatest place in the whole wide world."

"You're very kind." Galump showed her guests around the city. "It reminds us of simpler times."

"What times are those?" Arthur wanted to know.

"The time before *time* began," Galump said. She raised her mottled-green arm and pointed at her odd, water-filled wristwatch. "Before we invented clocks. Before we counted the days, the minutes, the seconds, the microseconds. Before we discovered words like *time* and *tide*."

"Oh," said Arthur, who didn't even own a wrist-watch, and who had a bad habit of being late for everything—except dinner, of course.

"Speaking of time," Galump said, "it's time for the Feast of Welcoming."

Which sounded just fine to Arthur, so long as he wasn't on the menu.

5

...

FEAST OF
THE FROG PEOPLE

ARTHUR'S ARRIVAL WAS celebrated in the Grand Hall, a place large enough to accommodate all of the Frog People, most of whom had never before seen a human.

"They think you're pretty special," Morf commented. He didn't sound particularly impressed himself.

"That's because I *am* special," said Arthur, preening a little as Galump's royal assistants carried him into the murky splendor of the Grand Hall. "There are thousands of them, and only one of me." It was such a novelty, being the center of attention—and not being made fun of—that he was determined to enjoy every moment of it.

The Grand Hall was an immense, underground cavern. Because it was located deep under the mud, there were no windows, and huge chandeliers hung from the vaulted ceilings. As he got closer, Arthur saw that the chandeliers were not powered by ordinary lightbulbs. The special bulbs were as large as goldfish bowls, and contained round, glowing sea creatures.

"Amazing," Arthur said, gazing up at the brightly glowing fishbulbs.

"Totally awesome," Morf agreed.

The banquet table was so long, Arthur couldn't see to the end of it. He was given the place of honor, a kind of throne made from a giant seashell. Meanwhile Morf perched on the arm of the throne and amused himself by making comments. "Quite the little family," he said, peering around with his bright, inquisitive eyes. "They don't call old Galump the queen mother for nothing. Everybody here is one of her children. Except us, of course. And I'm not so sure about you," he added.

"What do you mean?" Arthur asked in alarm.

"The Frog People all have sizable bellies, and so do you. So maybe you're a Frog Person, too."

"No way," Arthur protested. "I'm not in the least like a Frog Person. For starters, I don't have green-speckled skin."

"No?" Morf said. "Are you sure?"

Arthur looked down at his arms and was shocked to discover there were some green speckles on his skin from when he'd fallen on the pile of seaweed. But that didn't make him a Frog Person.

Galump signaled the start of the feast by ringing a small bell. It was made of clamshells and sounded very much like a wind chime. "Children!" she called out in her tubalike voice. "We are honored by the presence of something called Arthur, a human being from another world. Let us all welcome him and wish him good luck on his long and dangerous journey!"

With that, the mother of the Frog People bowed her great green head and made a deep, froglike noise: *ga-lump, ga-lump.* Her words were echoed by all the other creatures in the great hall, and when they spoke together the very air seemed to vibrate *GA-LUMP, GA-LUMP*, shaking the fishbulb chandeliers.

It was a strangely musical sound that Arthur could feel in the very pit of his stomach. What was she talking about—"dangerous journey"? Did that have something to do with not studying the instructions?

But suddenly Arthur felt very, very hungry, and compared to his hunger, nothing else mattered.

"Let the feasting begin!" Galump roared, and huge platters of food began to appear, passed from hand to hand until they filled the great banquet table. None of it looked anything like any food Arthur had ever seen before, but the delicious sea-salt smells made his mouth water.

"Ah!" said Morf, snatching a platter as it went by. "My favorite! Sea grapes!"

Arthur's diet was usually burgers and fries, but he was so famished, he munched happily on a bunch of the fruity things Morf called sea grapes. "Not bad," he said. "Not bad at all."

His experience with the sea grapes gave him the courage to sample tidbits from several of the other platters, and he discovered that everything was delicious. Ordinarily Arthur never ate vegetables if he could help it, but he didn't want the Frog People to think he was ungrateful, so he stuffed himself with various foods that resembled carrots and green beans, and he even ate a little of something that looked suspiciously like spinach.

The Frog People ate with great delicacy, patting their mouths with little green napkins. Meanwhile Morf, whose table manners left much to be desired, amused himself by flipping sea grapes into the air and catching them with his nimble tongue.

"Don't be a pig!" Arthur whispered urgently, embarrassed by Morf's behavior.

Morf burped and rolled his eyes. "You've got a lot of nerve," he said, "for someone with sea spinach all over his chin."

Mortified, Arthur hastily wiped his chin, but if any of the Frog People noticed, they didn't let on. Food kept coming down the endless banquet table for many hours.

Galump explained that she and her children normally ate only once a tide.

"Once a tide?" Arthur asked. "What does that mean?"

She tapped her water-filled wristwatch. "A tide is an interval of time. Here in REM World it compares to an interval you humans call a week."

"Ah!" he exclaimed, for that explained why the Frog People could eat for hours and hours—they must be very hungry if they only ate once a week. It also explained why Arthur was full to bursting and couldn't bear the thought of eating another bite.

Finally, after a dessert that looked suspiciously like snail Popsicles, Galump declared that the feast was at an end.

Morf nudged Arthur. "Are you ready?"

"Ready for what?" Arthur asked, somewhat alarmed.

In response, Morf burped. At first Arthur thought the little creature was being intentionally rude, but then the great dining hall began to echo with the sound of ten thousand burps.

In Mud City, burping was polite. "Come on, kid," Morf urged. "You can do it."

Arthur took a deep breath and clenched his stomach, and out came a really stupendous, mud-trembling *BUURRRRRRRRRRP!* that shook the very chandeliers.

His gigantic burp noise stunned the Frog People into silence. And then Galump put her green-speckled hands together and clapped. "Bravo!" she said, and a moment later, the thousands who had crowded into the Grand Hall erupted in wild applause.

"Arthur!" they chanted. "Arthur! Arthur!"

"Do they want me to make a speech?" Arthur asked Morf. He hoped not, since he'd never given a speech in his life and didn't want to start now.

"Another burp will do," said Morf. "But it has to be bigger and better, or don't bother at all."

As the Frog People waited expectantly, Arthur took another huge breath. He inhaled all the way into his stomach. Then he concentrated with all his might, and a massive, ear-splitting noise burst out.

BURRRRRRRRRRRRRRRRRRRRRRRRRRRRRRRRRRRRP!

Above him the fishbulbs shattered, dropping glowing sea creatures through the air, and the Frog People erupted into such a cacophony of cheering that the empty plates shook on the tables.

"You certainly know how to make an impression," Morf conceded when the cheering finally died down.

Galump smiled at him with her sad, wise eyes and rang her small clamshell bell. "Now is the time," she announced gravely, "for the viewing."

All at once a great silence settled over the hall, and Arthur realized that something really important was about to happen.

6

...

THE TROUBLE
WITH NOTHING

GALUMP BECKONED TO Arthur. "Come closer," she rumbled. "What I must show you looks small, although it is actually quite large."

"Is this a riddle?" asked Arthur. He hated riddles, mostly because he could never figure them out.

"See for yourself," Galump suggested, holding out her strange wristwatch.

The watch face was concealed by a beautiful white seashell. Galump flipped up the shell cover. Under the shell was what at first appeared to be a large, perfectly formed pearl the color of summer clouds. But when

Galump tapped the face of the watch, the clouds inside the pearl swirled away, revealing the darkness behind the sky.

"Sorry, but I can't see anything," said Arthur. He'd had similar problems looking through a microscope at school, when all he could make out was his own blurry thumb.

"Patience," Galump said soothingly.

Arthur looked into the strange wristwatch again, and this time he did see something. A shimmering inside the darkness. He bent down to get a closer look, and what he saw made his heart hammer inside his chest. "There's something inside the watch!" he exclaimed, unable to tear his eyes away.

"Take your time," Galump advised him. "Remember that watches are all about *time*."

The darkness behind the watch was so deep that Arthur felt as if he were looking down into a deep, dark mine shaft. A shaft so deep that light could never get all the way to the bottom. But something was rising up through the darkness. Something Galump wanted him to see.

Arthur gasped. "It's me!" he said.

Looking down into the face of Galump's mysterious wristwatch, Arthur saw a small, distinct image of himself lying on the workbench in the basement of his house. He was wearing the REM Sleep Device helmet, and he appeared to be deeply asleep. "What does it mean?" he asked, without taking his eyes from the watch.

"It means something has gone terribly wrong," Galump said gravely. Her mottled flesh had suddenly gone pale. "You're in two places at once, and that's supposed to be impossible."

"You mean I'm still asleep?"

"Part of you is," said Galump. "And part of you isn't. You're in violation of the laws of the universe! You must go home and set things right."

"You want me to go home?" asked Arthur. "But I like it here!"

Galump nodded wisely, and a little sadly. "You must go back to where you came from, or something terrible will happen. Indeed, it already may have started."

"I want to stay," Arthur said stubbornly. "I like Mud City. I like the Frog People and the way they burp after a meal. I even ate a piece of sea spinach, just to be polite!"

Galump reached out with her green-speckled arms and hugged Arthur. She smelled pleasantly of a salty, clean seashore. "We like you, too, little one," she said, patting his head. "But you must go back before it's too late."

"There's nothing wrong," said Arthur, looking around at this perfectly pleasant world. "It must be a mistake."

"Look again," said Galump softly, holding out her wristwatch.

So Arthur looked again. And this time he saw a strange kind of darkness seeping into the corners of the basement where his Other Self was lying unconscious on the workbench. The darkness looked like black, black water lapping in through the cracks in the floor and forming puddles, but somehow he knew it wasn't water. The creeping, liquid darkness made him deathly afraid, although he couldn't say why, exactly, except that something was wrong, terribly wrong.

"What is it?" he asked.

"The Nothing," Galump said.

"If it's nothing, then why does it matter?"

"Not that kind of nothing," Galump said. "Our legends tell us a thing called the Nothing existed before the creation of the Everything, and it's always out there, trying to force its way back to unravel the universe."

"But what's this got to do with me?" Arthur asked, frightened.

"There's another legend that one day something seemingly impossible will happen, that a crack will appear in the universe, and then the Nothing will seep in through the World Below."

Arthur was shocked and terrified. "This is so not fair!" he said. "All I wanted to do was lose weight, and now you're telling me the universe is going to end, and it's all my fault."

Galump looked deeply distressed. "I'm sorry, little one, but sometimes there are unexpected consequences for ordinary actions."

"But what do I do now?"

"Find a way home," Galump repeated. "If you're no longer in two places at once, that may stop the Nothing."

"But how do I get back?" Arthur asked, feeling terribly confused. "I forgot the stupid helmet, remember?"

"You go back by going forward," Galump told him.

"But that doesn't make any sense!"

"Here, borrow this," said Galump, strapping the mysterious watch to his wrist. "Now you will always know what time it is. And now it's time for you to move on. You won't be alone, little one. Morf is your guide. He can be an irritating animal sometimes, but we think you'll find him useful."

Suddenly a great bell began to chime.

DINGGGGGGG! DINGGGGGGG! DINGGGGGGG!

Arthur didn't know what the bell meant, but it was so loud, it had to be important. "What's wrong?" he cried.

"Nothing is wrong," Galump boomed. "The Great Bell is ringing because the tide has changed."

"Tide?" Arthur asked. "Changed?"

"The sea is returning to Mud City. It happens all

the time, and always right on time. There's nothing whatsoever to worry about. It's wonderful. Just remember to breathe underwater."

"But I can't breathe underwater!" Arthur exclaimed.

"Oh dear," said Galump. "I'd forgotten that about humans." And she sighed like the wind that stirs along a beach just before the tide comes in.

"May I make a suggestion?" Morf asked as he stood up on his hind legs and stretched.

"Yes," said Arthur.

"Run for your life!"

7

...

WATER, WATER, EVERYWHERE

THE FROG PEOPLE, thousands and thousands of them, streamed out into a square beside the mud-dribble castle. They were smiling, delighted that the tide was about to come back in, and they seemed hypnotized by the incoming waves.

Not even Galump took notice of Arthur anymore. It was as if he had vanished.

Arthur hurried to catch up with Morf, who was trotting along on all four legs, his tail straight up like a furry little flag. "What will we do?" Arthur asked.

"I only have one idea at a time," Morf purred. "And

right now my idea is *run for your life*. Unless, of course, you've got a better idea."

"I guess not," Arthur said, and he began to jog along as fast as he could. Which wasn't very fast at all.

The Great Bell went *DINGGGGGG! DINGGGGGG!* and the chime made him fear for his life.

"We'll never make it!" he shouted to Morf.

It was true. Already the horizon was starting to ripple with distant waves. He and Morf ran, and the hard mud splatted under their feet. Before long, the city of the Frog People was behind them, spires glinting in the sun of the bright green sky.

Arthur ran until he couldn't run anymore. Until his lungs hurt, and his legs ached, and his feet were hot. And, still, the rising water got closer and closer.

Finally he stopped and fell to his knees. He couldn't even complain about it, because he was panting so hard.

When Morf saw that Arthur couldn't take another step, he came back and sat down. He began to groom his tail. "Oh, well," the little creature said. "That's that, I guess."

Behind them the tide made a terrible splashing noise. Arthur's hair was ruffled by the wind that blew in front of the wall of water. Already Mud City had disappeared beneath the sea. In another moment they would disappear, too.

"I wish I could swim," Arthur said plaintively. Last

summer his mother had offered to take him for swimming lessons, but he had said no, certain that his appearance at the pool would have prompted a whole new slew of nicknames, like Whale Boy or, even worse, Leadbelly.

"Wishing won't work," Morf told him. "Maybe you could practice floating."

"I can't even float!" Arthur admitted bitterly. He knew, because he'd tried it in the bathtub and had gotten a mouth full of soapy water for his efforts.

"At least it's warm," Morf said. The water began to rise around their ankles.

"Aren't you ever afraid?" Arthur asked his new friend.

"Sometimes. When I'm afraid, you'll know we're in real trouble."

"Real trouble?" Arthur asked. The water now swirled up to his waist. "What do you call this?"

"A problem to be solved," Morf said, winking one of his big brown eyes. "I think I see the solution right over there."

The little creature pointed with his tail because his paws were already underwater. He was pointing at a white thing bobbing in the sea.

At first Arthur thought it was some kind of a sea monster. But as the thing swirled closer, Arthur saw that it was a small, battered boat.

Morf (who could swim quite nicely, thank you)

paddled over to the boat, clambered up the side, and steered it in Arthur's direction. "Climb in!" he urged. "There are more waves coming! Hurry!"

But poor Arthur could only hang on to the side of the boat. Climbing in was like doing a pull-up, and he couldn't do pull-ups, not even one. "Not even to save my life!" he told Morf. "Sorry, but I just can't, and that's all there is to it."

"Hard to believe," said Morf, his tail flicking with agitation. "A boy who can't even manage one pull-up. How did such a boy manage to get all the way to REM World? Hmmm? Because he gave up without trying? I don't think so."

"Sorry," Arthur said. His fingers started to slip. "Go on without me," he said bravely. "Save yourself."

Morf sighed, his eyes gazing back at the approaching waves. "Oh, well," he said. "I tried, even if you didn't."

"But I did try!" Arthur burbled as his mouth went underwater. "I—blub, blub, blub..."

"Look out!" Morf cried. "Shark! Shark!"

Before he knew what he was doing, Arthur pulled himself into the boat and lay gasping in the bottom. When he'd gotten his breath back, he said, "Now the shark will probably eat us, boat and all."

"Don't worry about the shark," Morf said loftily. "I was mistaken. There wasn't any shark."

"What!" Arthur sat up. He was furious.

"I see you managed to do a pull-up." Morf sniffed. "Now see if you can pull an oar. Quickly, or the waves will swamp us."

There wasn't time for Arthur to stay mad. He and Morf sat side by side on the only seat in the little boat, each holding an oar. Right behind them, a big wave was rising, threatening to break over the boat. The wave became larger and larger, until it seemed to fill the sky.

"Row!" Morf shouted.

"But I don't know how to row!" Arthur yelled. Which was absolutely true. He'd never rowed a boat in his life, so how was he supposed to learn now, with a giant wave about to crash over his head?

"Don't think about it!" Morf shouted. "Just do it!"

Arthur *wasn't* thinking about rowing. The wave was so big, it filled the inside of his mind, and there wasn't room for anything else. So he was completely surprised when Morf cried out, "Good! Keep it up!"

That's how Arthur discovered that his arms knew how to row, even if his brain didn't.

"Swing us around!" Morf shouted. "We have to face the wave!"

"But I don't want to *look* at the stupid wave!" Arthur screamed. The wave scared him so much, his knees felt like jelly. Nevertheless, he managed to turn the little boat around. The giant wave had risen up so high that the sky had grown dark. In another moment, the water would thunder down, smashing them into a zillion pieces.

"Hang on!" Morf shouted.

"I really don't want to see this," Arthur said, covering his eyes.

"Suit yourself," said Morf. He was standing on the seat, staring up at the very tip-top of the humongously huge wave. "I think it's actually as high as the clouds. Very unusual."

"Stupid wave!" Arthur cried, peeking through his fingers.

He heard Morf say, "Waves aren't stupid or smart. They just are."

And then their little boat began to rise. One moment they were at the very bottom of the wave, about to be buried under tons and tons of angry seawater, and the next moment the boat was shooting straight up into the sky.

"Elevator going up!" Morf shouted gleefully.

When Arthur had been much younger he had once ridden an elevator to the top of a very tall building. This felt like that, only much, much faster. So fast that Arthur's stomach seemed to plummet to the bottom of the sea while the rest of him shot straight up the face of the immense wave and was thrust nearly as high as the clouds.

"I told you so!" Morf said gleefully. "Wheeeeee! Let's do it again!"

But the giant wave passed beneath them and raced away to the other horizon, leaving a calm sea behind it. Morf was disappointed that there were no more giant waves to ride, but Arthur had almost passed out from relief, even if the experience had been sort of exciting, in a *scared-to-death* way.

"I'm *not* a boat kind of person," Arthur said.

"Could have fooled me," Morf chortled. "You rowed like a champ!"

"Really?"

Morf nodded. "Amazing what you can do if you don't think about it, huh? Pull-ups, rowing. I wonder what else you can manage?"

"I don't know," Arthur said. "The only thing I know is I'm supposed to go back home or the universe will end. At least that is what Galump says."

"Right," said Morf. "I almost forgot."

Morf settled down on the seat next to Arthur. "We'd better keep rowing," he said, picking up his oar.

And so they rowed and they rowed, and then they rowed some more. They rowed until the sun disappeared from the sky, and an emerald-green twilight spread like smoke across the sea, and then it was dark. Very dark.

"Where are we?" Arthur said with a sigh. "If we don't know where we are, how can we figure out where we're going?"

"No idea," Morf said. "Wish I knew, kid, but I don't."

The plain fact was, Arthur was lost. He was a million REM World light-years from home. At least. And he had no idea how to get back to where he'd started.

"It's no use," Arthur said, putting down the oar. He was so exhausted, he simply wanted to sleep.

"What's that?" Morf whispered, his ears twitching.

Arthur heard it, too. A soft, sighing sound that seemed to come from the edge of the world.

"Uh-oh," said Morf in a very small voice. And for the first time, he sounded afraid. Really afraid.

8

...

WIND OF
THE GIANTS

"WIND!" MORF CRIED. "It's coming to get us!"

Arthur listened again to the soft, sighing noise that seemed to come from the edge of the world. It didn't sound scary to him. "Just a little wind. What's the big deal?"

"The big deal is that it's a *big* wind," Morf told him. "It's the Wind of the Giants, and it knows we're out here in a leaky little boat in the middle of the ocean."

"Oh, baloney," said Arthur. "You're just tired. I get cranky when I'm tired, too."

But by the time he'd stopped talking, the wind was whipping at his hair and his clothes, and white froth was starting to form on the water. Morf wasn't just tired and cranky (although he had a right to be). This really *was* a big wind.

"Go away, you rotten old wind! You're nothing but hot air!" Arthur shouted. Or *tried* to shout, but the words were blown out of his mouth before he could say them.

Their little boat began to race along, running before the wind.

Now we're making progress, Arthur thought. At least they were going somewhere, even if they didn't know where somewhere was.

"Give me a hand!" Morf squeaked. He was trying to steer with an oar and was having a hard time of it.

Arthur tried to help steer with the oar, but it was no use. The boat went where it wanted to, racing along at an exhilarating speed, nearly as fast as the wind itself.

Looking up, Arthur saw the unfamiliar stars start to fade from the night sky. The first pale green blush of sunlight leaked up over the edge of the world. It was beautiful and terrifying at the same time.

"Look!" Morf cried. He pointed a trembling paw at the horizon. There, glinting in the light of dawn, jagged cliffs rose even higher than the big wave they'd managed to escape. "We're going to crash!"

Indeed, there was no way to avoid smashing into the base of the monstrous cliffs. They were going too fast to slow down, no matter how hard they tried to row in the opposite direction.

As the cliffs rose higher and higher above them,

and as Arthur and Morf prepared to crash, Morf hid under the seat and curled up with his tail over his eyes. He began to cry. "It was n-n-nice knowing you!" he called out to Arthur, his teeth chattering.

The idea of Morf shaking with fear made Arthur even more terrified. He thought about crawling under the seat also, but there wasn't room for both of them. In any case, Arthur felt it was his turn to act brave, even if he didn't feel it. "Don't worry," he said weakly. "We'll be okay." But he didn't believe it for a second.

He clutched the side of the boat and braced himself as the wind lifted them out of the water and hurled them through the air, right at the most jagged part of the terrible cliff.

This is the end, Arthur thought. He was about to close his eyes, when a dark shadow descended over them. The little boat was three feet away from being smashed into the cliff.

Then something snatched them right out of the air.

Something huge.

Something giant.

"Are we dead yet?" It was Morf's quavering voice under the seat.

"Not quite," said Arthur. And he nearly fainted.

• • •

Arthur was looking up into a face as big as a harvest moon. It was an old face, an ancient face, as weathered as the cliffs that rose up from the sea. Two great, bloodshot eyes studied the little boat. Each of the eyes was bigger than Arthur, and when he stood up in the boat to get a better look—he'd never seen a giant, after all—the enormous red eyes blinked slowly.

Morf crawled out from under the seat and looked up. "I knew it," he said softly. "I mean, it was obvious, wasn't it?"

"What are you talking about?" Arthur asked. *What could be less obvious than getting snatched up by a giant moments before being smashed to death?*

"This is what *always* happens when the Wind of the Giants blows you ashore," said Morf, disgusted. "He caused the whole problem! That's the point! Why couldn't that rotten giant just leave us alone? We could have rowed all the way home if he hadn't made the wind blow us here."

After the giant satisfied his curiosity about what the little boat looked like, he wanted to know what it smelled like.

Arthur looked up into a nostril as big as a mining tunnel.

The giant sniffed. Arthur and Morf had to cling to the boat or be sucked up his nose.

"This must be a good giant!" Arthur exclaimed. "He saved us, didn't he?"

"Of course he saved us," Morf complained indignantly. "He's hungry!"

And that's when the giant popped the little boat into his mouth and began to chew.

9

...

THE GIANT'S
TALE

"STOP!" BELLOWED Arthur at the top of his lungs.

Teeth as big as houses had already crunched the little boat to splinters, and Arthur and Morf clung precariously to the giant's slobbering lip.

"HUH?" the giant said.

An enormous finger cleared boat splinters from between his teeth, and Arthur and Morf found themselves dangling from the edge of a ragged fingernail.

The giant held them up for another look. After studying them for a moment he said, "FOOD!" and opened his mouth wide.

"Wait!" cried Arthur. Arthur knew what it was to

be hungry, so hungry you wanted to eat everything in sight. And that reminded him of the cookies in his pocket. With all the excitement that had happened so far in REM World, he'd forgotten about his stash of Oreos.

"I've got something that'll taste much better than us!" he shouted. And he held up a handful of cookies.

The giant was very hungry—his stomach was rumbling like an earthquake—but the cookies smelled interesting. Small, but interesting. "YOU ARE A HUMAN VISITOR TO REM WORLD?" he asked.

Arthur nodded.

Very delicately the giant took the cookies from Arthur's outstretched hand and placed them on the tip of his enormous tongue.

"UUUUMMMMMMMMM! GOOOOOOOOOOOD!"

And that is how Arthur Woodbury met the giant known as Grog, and came to hear the sad story of Grog's lonely life.

· · ·

Once he had decided not to eat Arthur and Morf, Grog turned out to be a gentle soul. He lived along the cliffs by the sea, where he used his strong breath of wind to bring him little things to eat. When he lay down to sleep (which happened only once every hundred years or so), he looked very much like a range of mountains. Trees grew on him while he slept, and when he snored, hurricanes devastated the coastlines.

"I AM GROG," he said. "LAST OF THE GIANTS. I AM ALONE. THERE IS NO OTHER."

His words boomed off the sea cliffs, causing small avalanches. But Arthur and Morf were safe in Grog's shirt pocket. Arthur found that the most comfortable place to sit was on top of Grog's pocket button, with his feet braced in the buttonhole. Morf relaxed in a shirt wrinkle, with only his tail showing.

"ONCE THERE WAS DROLL, BUT SHE IS NO MORE," Grog said sadly.

Tears rolled from his eyes and caused an unexpected rain shower far below.

"DROLL WAS THE LAST OF THE WOMEN GIANTS. I LOVED HER EVEN MORE THAN I LOVE TO EAT," said Grog.

"That's saying a lot," Morf sniffed.

"DROLL WAS THE MOST BEAUTIFUL WOMAN IN THE WORLD. HER GOLDEN HAIR WAS BETTER THAN SUNLIGHT, HER DRESS WAS A PRAIRIE OF GREEN, GREEN GRASS, AND HER EYES WERE LIKE BEAUTIFUL BLUE BEACONS FROM A NOBLE LIGHT-HOUSE, ALWAYS SHOWING ME THE WAY HOME.

"GROG STILL LOVES DROLL," he told them. "THESE WERE THE FIRST WORDS EVER SPOKEN, AND IT WAS SUMMER ALL OVER THE WORLD."

Grog asked Droll to be his wife, and she accepted the proposal and began to plan for the wedding, which was to take place in a thousand years or so.

That's right, a thousand years, for the wedding of giants takes a great deal of preparation. Just providing toothpicks means letting a forest grow to full maturity. Canyons have to be filled with champagne (the bubbles are *very* large) and cooled with the polar ice cap, which is an awkward task even for giants. The guest list alone fills all the books in the world, for every living creature is invited to a giant's wedding, and is expected to celebrate the event for at least ten generations.

Grog was at the South Pole, collecting ice for the champagne bucket, when disaster struck.

Droll, who could think of nothing but Grog and the upcoming wedding, went off in search of more flowers. A billion flowers simply wasn't enough, for there's no such thing as too many flowers at a wedding, and besides, she loved to hold buttercups under Grog's chin and watch his face shine.

In her search for more and better flowers, Droll traveled farther and farther from home. And one day she simply never came back.

When Grog returned with the polar ice cap— mighty proud of himself, was Grog—he expected to find Droll preparing a hot meal on the handy volcano she used for a stove. But the volcano was cold, and there was no sign of Droll.

Certain she would return any moment, Grog waited patiently for a year or so, and then he went looking. He searched high and low. He searched up above and down under. He searched inside and outside and even tried searching from the other side, but it did no good. Droll was gone.

She had vanished from the face of the planet, and he knew because he had searched every inch of it.

"What happened to her?" Arthur wanted to know.

Grog shrugged, which set off a series of minor earthquakes, because he'd been cooling his toes in the water far below. "MANY YEARS LATER, I HEARD THAT THE GROUND ITSELF OPENED BENEATH HER FEET, AND SHE FELL TO HER DOOM."

"Maybe she's still alive," Arthur suggested hopefully.

"IF SHE WAS ALIVE, I'D FEEL HER HEART BEATING. DROLL IS DEAD, AND I AM ALONE. AND WHEN I DIE, GIANTS WILL BE NO MORE."

Morf decided there had been quite enough talk about dying. "Tell me," he asked Grog, "have you found a helmet lying about? Arthur has lost his helmet, and if he doesn't find a way to get back home, the universe will end."

"THAT'S TERRIBLE," Grog boomed, setting off a thunderstorm. "I'VE NOT FOUND A LOST HELMET, OR IF I DID, I ATE IT BY MISTAKE."

Talking about eating something—even by mistake—made Grog hungry again, and he asked for more cookies.

Arthur was happy to give him some more.

"UUUMMMMMM! GOOOOOOOOOOOOOOOD!"

Grog added that he was sorry that he couldn't help Arthur find his way home, but he knew someone who might be of assistance.

"Oh?" piped up Morf. "And who would that be?"

"CLOUD PEOPLE," thundered Grog. "THEY KNOW EVERYTHING."

And so it was that Arthur Woodbury, the fat little kid everybody called Biscuit Butt, got to ride in a friendly giant's pocket, and climb to the very top of the world.

10

...

A SWOOP
OF WINGS

WITH HIS IMMENSE legs, Grog could cover a mile in a few strides, and he set off with a purpose. Soon the cliffs and the sea were far behind, and the giant was trodding through low mountain ranges that barely came up to his knees.

"What an incredible view!" Arthur exclaimed from Grog's pocket. "I've never been up in an airplane, but it can't be any better than this!" It was almost enough to make him forget that he was trapped in a world a million miles from home, and that his very life was in danger.

Deep inside the pocket, Morf said, "Ugh!"

"What do you mean, 'ugh'?" asked Arthur.

Morf groaned. "Motion sickness," he gasped. "I don't get seasick, but I do get giant sick."

"Raw deal," Arthur said sympathetically. "You're missing everything. Look! There's a flock of birds flying below us!"

"Oh no," groaned Morf. And then he made sick-making noises like a cat coughing up a very large hair ball.

· · ·

At first the low mountain ranges were covered with bristly trees, but as the mountains grew higher, the forest thinned out, and Arthur began to see bald patches on the mountaintops.

Grog had to slow down and wade through, for the mountains were waist-high, and he grumbled. "MOUNTAINS, MOUNTAINS, EVERYWHERE, AND EVERY PEAK IS BARE."

Before long the mountains got higher than Grog, and the giant had to climb over them. "HIGHER," he muttered, making the clouds tremble and weep with rain. "MUCH HIGHER."

Once, when he was particularly tired and hungry, Grog stopped and rested, wedging himself between two peaks. From a distance he looked like a mountain himself and, like these mountains, he was bald on top.

"MAY I HAVE ANOTHER COOKIE?" he asked.

Arthur was tempted to keep the last two for himself, because his stomach was growling. But it's not a good idea to deny cookies to a hungry giant, so Arthur dug deep in his pocket and gave Grog the last Oreos.

"MMMMMMM! GOOOOOOOOOOOOOOOOOD!"

Grog began to climb again, scaling his way up peak after peak, until they came to a mountain that was much, much larger than the others—a mountain that was as big to the giant as a regular mountain was to Arthur.

"HIGHER!" Grog thundered, causing lightning bolts to flash between his toes. "MUCH HIGHER!"

"How can we get higher?" Arthur asked Morf. "We're already way above the clouds."

"Don't remind me," Morf whimpered. His face was pale green.

"Maybe if you try holding your breath," Arthur suggested.

"That only works for hiccups. Is it much higher, do you think?"

"HIGHER!" said Grog. "MUCH HIGHER!"

The giant climbed and climbed. He climbed until he came to the highest clouds of all. Clouds so thick, the mist was like a soft, dense ceiling above the top of the world.

"HIGH ENOUGH FOR GROG!" he thundered, and far below, a glacier melted in fear.

"What happens now?" Arthur asked.

"UP YOU GO," Grog said, and he told Arthur and Morf to climb into his hand.

Grog clung to the steep mountain with his other hand and paused, bringing his enormous face down close to his two small friends. "BE CAREFUL," he said. "AND IF YOU EVER GET IN TROUBLE, ASK MORF TO CHANGE, AND HE WILL."

Arthur wanted to know what he meant about asking Morf to change, but before he could ask, the giant reached up, lifting them far into the highest clouds of all. The mist was so thick, they couldn't see the rest of the giant, only the hand that held them up.

Slowly the hand came to rest against a small ledge jutting out from the mountain.

"I guess this is where we get off," Arthur said uncertainly, helping Morf climb onto the ledge.

"I feel better already." Sure enough, Morf's face was no longer green.

"Good-bye, Grog!" Arthur shouted, his voice swallowed up by the mist below.

But the giant was already gone. They were alone, the two of them, stuck on a ledge many miles above the ground. And there was no way to get up or down.

"Do you think there's even a chance that I'll ever get home again?" Arthur asked. He was missing his mother and his grandmother. And he missed his refrigerator, always filled with delicious things to eat.

"It's not looking peachy just now," said Morf, looking around. "As a matter of fact, I'd *love* a peach. I'm famished." He stared at Arthur's pockets, hopefully.

"Sorry," said Arthur. "I gave the last cookie to Grog."

"That's the trouble with giants," Morf grumbled. "Oh, well, I suppose we'll just have to eat snow and pretend it's ice cream."

But there wasn't any snow. Just bare, unappetizing rock.

"I'm not hungry enough to eat a rock," Morf said. "Not yet."

"Ssssh!" Arthur hissed. "Did you hear that?"

"Hear what?" Morf asked.

Then he heard it, too.

SWOOOOOOP...SWOOOOOOP...SWOOOOOOP.

The swoop of wings.

11

. . .

THE CLOUD
PEOPLE

ARTHUR AND MORF huddled together as the sound
of swooping wings got closer and closer. They could
see nothing through the mist, but something was certainly approaching.

"I hope it's not a pterodactyl," said Arthur.

"What's a pterodactyl?" Morf asked, worried.

"You don't want to know."

Arthur squinted, trying to make out whatever it
was that was swooping through the clouds. But it was
no use. Maybe he was hearing things.

"Look out!" cried Morf. Something was taking
shape in the mist.

At first it looked like a very large bird, gliding on the updrafts, but as the thing drew closer, Arthur saw that it was not a bird at all. It was human-shaped, with wide, delicate wings. A moment later it perched on the edge of the ledge and looked at him with startled eyes.

"What are you?" it said.

Except for the wings, which swept from its wrists to its ankles like the wings of a large, pale bat, it looked like a girl about Arthur's age. Its voice trembled, and Arthur realized that the flying girl creature was even more frightened than he was.

"I'm Arthur Woodbury," he said, trying very hard to sound casual. "I'm a visitor here, and this is my guide, Morf."

Morf switched his tail and bowed, and something about the way he did it made the girl creature giggle. She covered her mouth with one hand, but her eyes—quite beautiful eyes, Arthur thought—were still laughing.

"Oh," she said. "I've never seen an Arthur or a Morf. You both look so funny! Where have you come from? What are you doing here? Where are your wings?"

Her name was Leela, and she had a hundred questions. Arthur did his best to answer them all, although the more he told her about his journey to REM World, and whatever had gone wrong back home, the more she became confused.

"The World Below? There's nothing beneath the clouds, and I should know, because I've flown lower than any of the others."

"Others?" Arthur asked. "What others?"

"Why, the other Cloud People, of course."

"That's odd," Arthur mused. "Grog said the Cloud People know everything, but you don't seem to know much at all."

Leela stood up straight and gave him a defiant look. "How dare you speak to me that way! Do you know who you're talking to?"

"I, um, guess not," Arthur stammered.

"When I grow up, I shall be the Cloud Master—the *leader* of the Cloud People! So there!"

Morf tugged at Arthur's sleeve. "Ask her if there's a way off this ledge," Morf whispered. "But be nice, or she'll fly away."

As nicely as he could, Arthur asked.

Leela seemed pleased by the question, perhaps because she knew the answer. "Of course there is. What good would a ledge be without a way off?"

"I'm sure I don't know," said Arthur.

"Ha! For all your criticisms of me, *you* don't know much, do you? For your information, the way off a ledge is always up, never down."

Leela led them to the back of the ledge and showed them where narrow steps had been carved into the rock. "It looks awfully steep," Arthur said, gazing up into the mist.

But Morf was already scampering up the steps, and in two shakes of his tail, he disappeared into the clouds above. Arthur decided if Morf could do it, he could, too, and he began to climb, staying close to the face of the mountain.

One wrong step, and he knew he wouldn't stop falling until he hit bottom, miles and miles below.

"Hurry up," Leela said. She was right below him. She climbed the steep, steep stairs as if she didn't have a care in the world.

"But you've got wings!" Arthur protested. "It doesn't matter if you fall. If I fall, it's splat city."

"What's a city?" Leela asked.

Rather than try to explain, he said, "Oh, never mind."

"Hurry," she insisted, nudging his foot. "I want to show you something."

Arthur was too nervous and out of breath from climbing to ask her about it, and Leela didn't bother to explain. She seemed to think that Arthur should know all about the Cloud People, even though she obviously knew nothing about *him*.

When at last Arthur reached the top of the incredibly steep and dangerous precipice, he was so exhausted, all he could do was flop on the ground. He lay there gasping like a fish out of water.

Leela shook her head. "You're the strangest creature I've ever seen."

"I'm not a creature," Arthur protested. "I'm a boy."

"Then 'boys' must be very strange creatures," said Leela. "Come along. You'll love what I'm going to show you. But we need to hurry."

She took Arthur's hand and helped pull him to his feet. He looked around for Morf, but the mist was so thick, he couldn't see much of anything.

We're inside a cloud, Arthur thought. And he was right.

"It must be very odd not having wings," Leela said as she tugged him along. "How do you fly?"

"I don't."

Leela looked at him, shocked. And then tears welled up in her beautiful eyes. "That's the saddest thing I ever heard. Are you sure?"

"Of course I'm sure," said Arthur.

He'd never even thought about having wings, but Leela's tears made him feel sad, too. And he sniffled a little, feeling sorry for himself. It didn't seem fair that some creatures were thin and born with wings and lived in the air, and others—the fat Arthurs of the world—had to trudge along the surface of things.

"We made it," Leela said, and her face lit up with a smile. "We're just in time."

Arthur started to say, "Just in time for what?" when he looked up to find that he was surrounded by Cloud People.

As the mist cleared away he saw dozens of them,

standing with great dignity upon a flat, rocky precipice. Their wings were wrapped around them like pale robes. Like Leela, they had large, beautiful eyes, and each appeared to be staring with reverence at the setting sun.

Below them the clouds were so puffy and thick that Arthur thought for a moment he might walk across the mist-filled gulf to the next precipice. Fortunately he thought the better of it, for had he done so, this story would have ended right here, and Arthur would still be falling.

"Hello," Arthur said, wanting to be polite.

"SILENCE."

The word came from the tallest of the Cloud People, who stood at the farthest edge of the precipice. In a gentler voice he said, "Our Mother the Sun is about to die, and Her spirit will go far, far below. Each night She dies. Each day She is reborn as morning. Her warmth makes the clouds, and the clouds make us. Let us give thanks to our Mother."

At that moment, just as the sun was about to go down, the Cloud People unfurled their wings. They looked like flowers opening their petals. The last rays of the sun made their wings transparent, and Arthur thought he had never seen anything so beautiful.

"*Thank you, Mother,*" they sang softly, and Arthur could see that it was a kind of prayer, and he bowed his head out of respect.

The clouds glowed with the fading light of the setting sun, and the pale green sky began to fill with the unfamiliar stars of REM World. Which reminded Arthur that he was a long, long way from home, and that he still had no idea how to get back there.

He was just starting to feel terribly homesick and worried, when something tugged at his hand.

"How much time do we have left?" Morf asked.

"What?" Arthur asked.

"Time," Morf repeated. "How much is left before it runs out?"

"Before what runs out?"

"Time," Morf repeated.

"How should I know?" Arthur said irritably.

"Check your watch," Morf suggested, tapping his wrist.

The watch. Of course! Arthur had forgotten all about the special wristwatch Galump had given him.

With trembling fingers he lifted the seashell cover and looked into the dark abyss.

12

...

NO ONE KNOWS EVERYTHING

ARTHUR SHIVERED, FEELING much more frightened than he had been while climbing the perilous precipice, or running from the tide, or hanging from the giant's slobbering lip. Looking into the face of the watch, he had that terrible falling feeling you get in a dream, except the feeling didn't stop, even though he was wide awake.

"I wish I knew what went wrong," he said. "If I knew what was wrong, I could fix it."

Inside the watch face, suspended in darkness, he saw his Other Self sound asleep on the workbench.

The REM Sleep Device covered his head. The entire floor of the basement was flooded with liquid darkness, rising like the darkest water imaginable, lapping at the legs of the workbench where his Other Self slept on, unaware.

He wanted to yell, "Wake up!" but somehow he knew it wouldn't work.

"What's wrong?" Leela asked. She was peering over his shoulder and saw the strange, seashell watch strapped to his wrist.

Leela seemed so concerned that Arthur decided to let her peer into the watch and see what he saw. When she caught sight of the liquid darkness flooding into the basement, she gasped, and her hands flew to her mouth. "Not that!"

"Not what?" Arthur asked. "What do you know about the Nothing? Do you have any idea how I can get back home?"

Leela shook her head sorrowfully. "You must speak to my father."

As the stars grew brighter in the sky, the Cloud People wrapped themselves up in their beautiful wings and gathered around Arthur and Morf.

"You are not of our world," the Cloud Master said gravely. "Do you come from the World Below?"

Arthur was about to answer, when Leela interrupted. "Don't be silly, Father. There's no such thing as the World Below. That's just a story for children."

"Hush, my daughter," said the Cloud Master. "Because you have not seen a place does not mean it doesn't exist."

The Cloud Master then invited Arthur and Morf into his home, which was a kind of cave carved into the face of the precipice. The interior was lit by many small candles suspended from the ceiling. It was like having the night sky inside your house, for the candles twinkled like stars.

"Very cozy," whispered Morf as he curled up on a footstool.

Leela (who hadn't said a word since her father told her to hush) set about preparing food for the visitors. The Cloud Master watched his daughter with an expression of great affection. "Leela is the master of this house," he explained. "It has been so since her mother died. My daughter has many strong opinions, which is to be expected in one so young, but she is wrong in her thoughts about the World Below. If there is no World Below, how can there be a World Above?"

"Very wise," Morf commented. "Grog the Giant told us the Cloud People know everything. He must have been talking about you."

The Cloud Master stared at the furry little creature casually lounging on his footstool, and then he burst out laughing. "Indeed? Is that our reputation? Remarkable! There are very old legends about Grog the Giant, but I had no idea he still existed. Was it he who brought you to the World Above?"

"Yes!" Arthur and Morf said together.

"Then I will try to be wise," said the Cloud Master, ruffling his wings and sitting up straighter. "But I warn you, in spite of what Grog told you, there are many things I don't know. No one knows everything; that is one of the things I do know. It was a hard lesson, because when I was Leela's age, I *did* know everything, but as I get older I know less and less."

Listening to the Cloud Master speak made Arthur feel a little dizzy. Or maybe it was just hunger, because he was very hungry indeed. He hadn't had a thing to eat since the feast in the Grand Hall, and his stomach was so empty, it kept rumbling, "Feed me! Feed me!"

Leela, still maintaining her silence, brought out covered trays of food, and Arthur eagerly lifted the lids. He was greatly disappointed to discover the trays were empty.

"Help yourselves," the Cloud Master said. "My daughter is a wonderful cook."

"But there's nothing there!" Arthur burst out.

The Cloud Master laughed. "Nothing you can see. But just because you can't see it, doesn't mean it's not there. Look again."

Arthur did as he was told, and this time he saw a faint, cloudy mist rising from the tray. He put his finger in the mist, and sure enough, something was there. It felt like Jell-O, only less solid. Cautiously he lifted his finger to his mouth.

"Delicious!" was all he could bring himself to say, because he was too busy scooping up the rest of the nearly invisible meal.

It tasted like nothing he had ever tasted before. Like sponge cake that was lighter than air, but different. It wasn't sweet or sour or bitter. It didn't taste like fruit or vegetable, meat or dairy.

It tasted, Arthur finally decided, like clouds.

"Eat your fill," the Cloud Master urged him.

Arthur was thrilled. Meanwhile, Morf lapped at his tray and purred with contentment.

As they dined, the Cloud Master spoke about his people.

"Our legends are very important to our people. They are the keys to the truths we know. They tell us that the first of us came from the World Below. We had no wings then, no power of flight. But we did have enemies—four-legged beasts with mighty fangs—and the beasts chased us into the sky. Which means, I think, that many thousands of years ago, our ancestors began migrating into the mountains, looking for a safe place to live. As you know, it is very difficult to survive up here unless you fly, and after much hardship and many generations, our ancestors were given the gift of flight.

"But as you see," the Cloud Master said, unfurling

his wings, "we are not birds. We cannot simply flap off a perch and fly wherever we desire. We must glide and soar, using the air and the wind to lift us. If I should venture to glide too low beneath the clouds," he said, cutting a look at his daughter, "I might never be able to get back to the World Above. I would be lost, spiraling down and down. Even if I survived, I would have to spend the rest of my life in the World Below and walk upon the ground as the other creatures do."

"Like us," Morf piped up.

The Cloud Master coughed delicately. "Well, yes," he admitted. "Like you. I mean no offense, but for those of us born with flight, life on the ground is unimaginable."

"I wish I had wings," said Arthur wistfully. "If I had wings, I'll bet I could find my way home."

"Is that why you came to the World Above? To find your way home?" the Cloud Master asked.

Arthur explained, as best he could, what had happened after he had come up out of his own basement and found himself in another world. How he'd met Morf and how he'd been taken in by the Frog People. When he mentioned the problem with the liquid darkness leaking into his basement, the Cloud Master looked as if he'd been slapped in the face.

"The Nothing!" he exclaimed. "It can't be!"

"See for yourself," said Arthur, holding out the wristwatch.

The Cloud Master studied the image lurking inside the wristwatch. When he saw that the liquid darkness was still there, flooding into the basement where Arthur's Other Self slept on, oblivious to danger, he groaned and covered the watch face.

"It's true," he said. "The Nothing has found a way in. What else did the Frog People say?"

"They said if I got back home then I wouldn't be in two places at once, and the Nothing would stop rising."

The Cloud Master nodded. "The Frog People must be very wise. We, too, have legends about the Nothing. It is said that one day the Nothing will leak into our world, and every world, and it will keep on filling up the universe until all the stars go dark, and then Everything will cease to exist. The universe, all life, all light, will be no more. Of course it may only be a legend. Maybe what we see in the watch is simply an illusion."

"Oh, I hope so!" Arthur said. "Maybe it doesn't matter if I didn't read the instructions and left that stupid helmet behind!"

Leela rattled a tray impatiently. She had been forbidden to talk, so all she could do was rattle the dishes and scowl until her father finally paid attention.

"Yes, my dear," he said kindly. "Of course you may speak, assuming, of course, that you have something to say."

"I have something to say, all right!" Leela said

hotly. "And what I say is this: The Nothing isn't a legend or a fairy tale. The Nothing is real. I saw it only yesterday! I didn't know what it was at the time, but now I'm sure. That's why I thought the World Below didn't exist. Because the Nothing is already here!"

For once, the Cloud Master was speechless.

"Please," Arthur asked. "Tell us what you saw."

And so she did.

13

...

WHAT
LEELA SAW

"OF ALL THE CLOUD PEOPLE, I am the best flyer," Leela said calmly. The candlelight made her eyes sparkle. "I know where all the updrafts are, and how to use the rising air to soar as high and as far as any of the Cloud People have ever flown.

"Ever since I was a small child, I have heard the legends of the World Below," she continued. "Yesterday morning, I decided to go look for it with my own eyes—"

"Leela!" her father interrupted. On his face was an expression of great concern. "It is forbidden! You know that!"

"Nevertheless," said Leela, "I was determined. And

the winds from below were especially favorable, so I set off with three of my friends—"

"Leela! You endangered your friends? How could you do such a thing?"

"Father, may I continue?" Leela said it patiently, as if she had expected him to keep interrupting.

"Of course," he said with a sigh.

"We dared each other. Who was brave enough to venture to the World Below? Each of us spoke of our courage, but none of us wanted to go alone. So we decided to go together. And we did. I led the way, soaring out to the great cloud canyons of the east, where the mountains are steepest. The clouds were thin yesterday morning, and we could see down many miles. We circled lower and lower. And four of us were frightened, but no one spoke of fear. We knew that we must find powerful updrafts, or we could never return to the World Above."

"Oh, Leela," whispered her father. "How could you?"

"One by one my friends gave up, catching updrafts and returning to the height of the sky. I didn't blame them for being afraid, because I was afraid, too. But something inside me wanted to see the World Below even more than it wanted to give up and go home. And so I continued to spiral down. I flew lower, still, into an area of twilight, where the peaks of the mountains block the light of the sun—"

"No one has ever flown that low!" Her father was clearly anguished.

"I have," Leela told him. "I flew that low and much lower, too. Because I could see something deeper still, far below the shadows of twilight. Something that seemed to know I was there. Something that beckoned me. Something that whispered inside my head, like the faintest whisper of wind."

"Our legends speak of those voices!" her father cried. "They issue from Vydel's Mouth, at the very bottom of the World Below."

"Yes," said Leela. "And the voices seemed to be saying, 'Come to us. Come to us and be happy. Come to us and stay forever.' The voices frightened me even more than the fear of never getting back to the World Above. So I leveled off my flight and soared over a great chasm. A chasm opening out of the darkness, with giant stone pyres that rose like the white fangs of some terrible beast."

"Vydel's Mouth!" her father exclaimed. "You saw it!"

"Yes. But deep inside it, I saw something worse. Much worse."

Leela paused, and Arthur and Morf leaned forward expectantly, as if they both knew what she was about to say.

"I saw the Nothing," she said quietly. "It bubbles up from the chasm—from what the legends call Vydel's Mouth—and it floods out over the very bottom of the world. And where the Nothing touches, nothing remains. That is why I told you that the World Below does not exist. Because the part I saw—the very lowest part—exists no longer."

"It is the beginning. of the end," her father said with great sadness. "The Nothing has found a way in."

"How did you get back?" Arthur asked eagerly.

"I circled above the chasm for many hours. Never dipping any lower, but never getting any higher, either. Finally, at the very edge of the chasm, I came upon a faint updraft. I could feel the warmth of it under my wings, and it carried me upward. When the updraft faded, I veered as close to the mountains as I dared, and there I found another updraft. And another. Eventually I was lifted out of the shadows and into the sunlight, and then it was easy to find the rising air. At last I came to this very precipice, and knew I'd finally made it home. I wept like a child. And then, today, I found Arthur."

Leela sat with her hands folded, waiting for her father's reaction. He stared solemnly at her for a long time, and then he sighed deeply. "You are no longer a child. That should have been obvious to me, I suppose. But it is never easy for a father to watch his daughter grow up."

"You'll always be my father," Leela said softly. "That will never change."

The Cloud Master opened his wings and wrapped them around Leela. "And you are the best daughter ever," he said.

Arthur heard someone sobbing.

It was Morf. Tears were streaming from his large brown eyes. "Don't mind me," the little creature said. "I always cry when I'm happy."

"Happy! The Nothing is going to eat up the whole universe. How can you be happy?" Arthur demanded.

Morf wiped away a tear and then looked Arthur right in the eye. "Because you're going to stop it," he said. "That's why."

14

...

THE LEGEND
OF THE END
OF THE WORLD

"BUT I DON'T KNOW how to get home!"
Arthur exclaimed.

Morf shrugged his furry little body, as if that was
the answer he expected to hear.

"Silence!" said the Cloud Master. In his voice was
such authority that all of them immediately grew still.

In the silence, Arthur watched the star-twinkle of
the candles, and he also watched the Cloud Master,
who closed his eyes and was obviously deep in
thought.

When he spoke at last, the Cloud Master was so
quiet, Arthur had to listen very, very hard.

"There is another legend," he began. "A legend so terrible that we do not speak of it. It is the legend of the end. It is about the visitor who will come from another world. It is said that the Nothing will follow him. It is also said that this visitor has two choices. The first is to do nothing, and if he does nothing, the end must come. The Nothing will rise and devour everything, even the clouds in the sky, and the Cloud People will be no more.

"The visitor's second choice is to do battle with the Nothing, and in some versions of the legend, the visitor wins. In other versions, he fails, and the end comes even sooner."

The Cloud Master paused, waiting until silence again filled the chamber. "Which do you choose?" he asked, looking directly at Arthur.

"How can I choose when I don't know what to do?" asked Arthur, who was more confused now than he had ever been in his life. "First the Frog People tell me I must find a way home. Now you tell me I must do battle with the Nothing and, even if I do, I might fail."

"It is very difficult," the Cloud Master agreed. "But if my understanding of the legend is correct, there is only one way to find your way home."

"How do I get there?"

"Through Vydel's Mouth," the Cloud Master said.

"I might have known," Arthur said sarcastically. "Naturally it would be someplace impossible."

"Not quite impossible," the Cloud Master corrected him. "There is a way for you to enter Vydel's Mouth."

"What way is that?" Arthur asked, even though he was afraid to hear the answer.

"You must learn to fly."

. . .

It was time to sleep.

Arthur was so perplexed and excited at the idea of learning to fly that he was sure he'd never sleep again. But when Morf curled up beside him on a blanket made of the softest down imaginable, Arthur's eyelids grew heavy, and he was soon fast asleep.

In his dreams, he floated through the sky, eating small, delicious clouds that tasted like pancakes. And the more he ate, the thinner he got.

. . .

Leela woke him before dawn. "We mustn't be late," she said. "Being late for sunrise brings the worst kind of luck."

Arthur was shivering when he got up. Nights were cold at the top of the world, and as soon as he stood up, he missed the comforting warmth of the blanket. He made the mistake of saying so.

"Oh, bring the blanket if you're going to be such a sissy," Leela said in a huff. "But whatever you do, hurry!"

Arthur followed her out of the cave, wearing the blanket like a robe of wings. His breath made little clouds in the starlight.

"Brrrr!" said Morf. "I'm glad I've got fur!"

"I wish *I* had fur," Arthur muttered. He felt ridiculous wrapped in the blanket, but he still wasn't willing to leave it behind.

The Cloud Master had assembled his people at the edge of the precipice. Arthur was relieved to see that he wasn't the only one shivering. He didn't know what was dumber: getting up before the sun or going outside when it was so cold it made your nose numb.

He was thinking about sneaking back to bed, when all of a sudden the sky changed. One moment a billion stars twinkled like diamonds in the sky; then a flash of pale green light suddenly washed away all but the three brightest stars.

"It begins!" the Cloud Master called out, raising his arms wide. "Morning is born!"

A blaze of orange sliced along the horizon like a hot knife. As sleepy and cold as he was, Arthur had to admit it was a beautiful sight. The sun really did look as if it had just been born, climbing fresh and new out of the darkness, making the whole sky glow with the promise of life.

"Our Mother has risen," the Cloud Master announced. "Her warmth makes the clouds, and the clouds make us. Let us give thanks to our Mother."

"Thank you, Mother," his people sang.

The Cloud People slowly unfurled their wings, which glowed like flower petals in the pale green light of the rising sun. Without thinking about it, Arthur spread wide his arms and let the blanket fall away, as if he, too, were opening his wings. He felt lighter than he'd ever felt before. Light enough to fly, if only he knew how.

"Don't get any crazy ideas," Morf whispered. "There's no such thing as a flying biscuit."

"What are you talking about?" Arthur asked.

"I noticed the gleam in your eye," Morf said. "Like you thought you were lighter than air."

"Oh, shut up," Arthur said.

"Fine," said Morf, folding his little arms.

And that's when Leela and the Cloud Master came over and told him it was time.

"Time for what?" Arthur asked.

"Time to learn how to fly," Leela told him.

"Or die trying," the Cloud Master added.

15

...

THE BOY WITH
THE BLANKET

"First you must be strong," the Cloud Master told him. "Strong enough to lift your own weight."

"Oh no," said Arthur despondently, because he knew what that meant. Pull-ups. And he couldn't do even one pull-up. Every time he had tried and failed, the other children had given him a new nickname. Fat Boy, Lardo, Jelly Belly, it never seemed to end.

"Sorry, but I can't do pull-ups," Arthur said in a small voice.

"Nonsense," Morf snapped, flicking his furry tail. "You pulled yourself into the boat when I yelled, 'Shark!'"

"That only works if I believe it."

"Then believe it," the Cloud Master said ominously. "Go on, try."

The Cloud Master held out one of his arms, indicating that Arthur should grab hold and use it as a chinning bar.

"But I can't," Arthur whined.

"No whining," said the Cloud Master. "Just do it."

Arthur tried, but he couldn't budge himself from the ground.

"Try the feather," the Cloud Master suggested to Leela.

Leela grinned. She produced a small feather and began to tickle Arthur's ankles. Arthur hated to be tickled, and he started to kick. Before he knew it, his chin was over the Cloud Master's arm.

"Splendid," said the Cloud Master. "Now try it without the feather."

"Oh please, Father," Leela protested. "I love tickling him. Look at him squirm."

"Leela!"

She sighed and put the feather away.

Arthur pulled himself up. It wasn't really that difficult, for some reason. "Maybe I'm lighter up here at the top of the world," he said.

"Come on, do another," said the Cloud Master. "Very good. Another."

And Arthur managed to chin himself eleven times

before his fingers slipped and he fell to the ground. He was so pleased that he didn't mind landing smack on his backside.

"He can't be Mr. Biscuit anymore," Morf decided. "The boy needs a new name."

"Excellent idea," said the Cloud Master. "Any suggestions?"

Morf gave it some thought. "The Wingless Wonder?"

"More like the Brainless Wonder," Leela muttered.

"No, no," the Cloud Master said, rubbing his chin. "He needs a proper name. Never mind. It will come to me."

"We could call him Rocks-In-His-Head," Leela muttered. "Or Pancake."

"Watch your tongue, young lady," said the Cloud Master sternly.

When her father wasn't looking, Leela stuck out her tongue and pretended to look at it. Which made her beautiful eyes cross, and that got Arthur laughing.

"You must run before you can fly," said the Cloud Master. "Run, the both of you. As far and as fast as you can go."

"But, Father!"

"You heard me," the Cloud Master said. "Run!"

"But I hate running!" Arthur protested.

"Even better," said the Cloud Master. "Run until you don't hate it anymore."

Arthur was determined not to run—running was so

stupid—but when Leela started chasing him with the feather, what choice did he have? He lumbered along, puffing and panting, and each time she touched him with the feather, he went a little faster. He hated being tickled even more than he hated running.

"Take that!" Leela squealed, tickling him on the back of his neck. "And that!" Her feather found a most sensitive spot behind his left ear.

She chased him clear around the precipice, and then up a trail carved into the rock. They ran down another trail, and after a while Arthur decided it was sort of fun being chased by a wild, beautiful girl creature. Once, he managed to pull away from her, running for all he was worth, but she opened her wings and swooped high up into the sky. He lost sight of her in the sun, and then when he looked again, there she was, blocking his way.

"Gotcha!" she shrieked, and tickled his nose.

Arthur ran in the opposite direction, and it took Leela a long time to catch up. "Slow down!" she called out, sounding disappointed.

"No way!" he shouted back. He raced down the trail, back to the flat area of the precipice. He was running so hard that at first he didn't notice all the Cloud People gathered there. And when they began to applaud, he was really mystified.

"Hurrah for Arthur! Hurrah for the boy from the World Below!"

They were cheering for him.

The Cloud Master held up Arthur's hand. "No one has ever outrun Leela," he explained. "You have proven your strength and your speed, and now it is time to see if you can fly."

"But how can I fly without wings?" Arthur wanted to know.

"Close your eyes," the Cloud Master commanded. Such was the power of his voice that Arthur instantly obeyed.

With his eyes closed, Arthur felt something touch his back, just between his shoulder blades.

"Hold up your arms," the Cloud Master said. "Now open your eyes."

When Arthur opened his eyes he saw that wings were now attached from his wrists to his shoulder blades. The wings had been cleverly fashioned out of the blanket he'd slept in, and he held them up for the crowd to admire.

"What beautiful wings! They're as good as real!"

Arthur had always thought of himself as fat and ugly, but the blanket-wings made him feel handsome for the first time in his life. Even Morf looked impressed.

"Not bad," said the little creature, looking him over. "Not bad at all."

Eager to take flight, Arthur flapped his new wings. He flapped very hard, but nothing happened.

Leela laughed. "You'll never fly that way," she said. "Cloud People don't flap. We're not birds. We glide and soar."

Arthur was mortified. He had wanted to take off like an eagle and impress everyone with his strength and skill. And here he was flapping his arms like a doodlebrain. Looking, no doubt, like a tubby boy with a blanket pinned to his shoulders. He wanted to crawl under a rock and disappear, but everyone was watching him, and there was no escape.

"Come with me," the Cloud Master commanded.

He took Arthur's hand and led him to the very edge of the steepest cliff. Far below, the clouds looked like puffy waves on a sea of air. A warm wind ruffled Arthur's hair, and despite the warmth, he shivered.

"I'm afraid," he whispered.

"And so you should be," said the Cloud Master. "Flying is the second most dangerous thing in the world."

"What's the first most dangerous thing?"

"Falling."

"I can't fly," Arthur said, and his voice trembled with fear. "I'm just a boy with a blanket."

The Cloud Master gave him a solemn look. "You are not *just* anything. You are whatever you think you are. What you *believe* yourself to be. Are you a boy with a blanket? Or are you a boy who can save the universe?"

Arthur gulped.

Behind him, Leela piped up. "Let me show him, Father! Let me show Arthur how to fly!"

The Cloud Master was about to tell his daughter to hush, but then he thought better of it. "Good idea," he said.

Leela took Arthur's hand. "Hold your arms out like this," she said. "The wind will lift you."

With Leela holding his hand, Arthur felt less afraid. "I'm ready," he said.

And he stepped off the edge of the cliff, into the air.

16

. . .

LEAP
OF FAITH

HE FELL LIKE a rock. Headfirst, straight down the face of the steepest cliff. He fell so fast that his stomach was left behind. The wind brought tears to his eyes.

Beside him, Leela fell, too.

"When I say, 'NOW!' lift up your arms and arch your back!" she yelled, shouting above the wind.

They fell so far and so fast that before Arthur could even think about it, they plunged into the layer of fluffy clouds that had seemed miles below.

Arthur had hoped the clouds would be thick enough to slow them down, but it wasn't like that. If anything, falling through the mist was more horrifying because he couldn't tell where the ground was, or how soon he would get there.

Beside him Leela yelled, "Wait! Wait!" Then she shouted, "NOW!" As soon as the word was out of her mouth, she popped her wings and shot up, as if yanked by a string.

Arthur knew it was hopeless, but he did as she'd told him. He lifted his arms and arched his back.

Suddenly he wasn't falling quite so fast. His blanket-wings filled with rushing air, and he could feel himself slowing down.

"MORE!" Leela shouted from above. "MORE!" So he arched his back some more and lifted his arms as far as they would go.

He was still falling, but not as fast as before.

Leela swooped below him and turned over on her back. "Like this!" she yelled, and then she tilted her wings and rose, soaring on an updraft.

As best he could, Arthur tried to mimic what she'd done. It wasn't easy, but when he turned his wrist and tightened the blanket-wings, he could feel the air trying to lift him.

"You're flying!" Leela yelled from directly above him.

Arthur tightened the blanket-wings even more. He swooped upward uncertainly and bumped into Leela, who laughed with delight. "That's it!" she cried. "You've got it!"

Playfully she pulled away from him. Arthur followed.

"This is so cool!" he cried. "Flying is the coolest thing in the whole wide world!"

"This way!" Leela called out, and she disappeared into the mist.

Arthur turned his arms and banked, blanket-wings fluttering. Leela was there, waiting, her eyes shining with excitement. "Follow me!" she said.

Slowly Arthur and Leela rose up out of the layer of clouds, but they were still far below the World Above. "There's an updraft at the face of the cliff!" Leela told him. "We need to find it!"

She swooped away again, her pale wings glowing in the sunlight. Arthur struggled a bit, but he managed to keep up with her.

All of a sudden the face of the steepest mountain was right before them, and Arthur had to raise his arms to prevent himself from crashing into it.

"Here it is!" Leela announced. "Lift your head and fly!"

And with that, she was lifted straight up the face of the cliff.

"Wait for me!" Arthur called out, and at that very moment he felt the warm updraft under his blanket wings. He shot up the side of the mountain, craning his neck to catch sight of Leela, who kept urging him upward.

"Fly!" she kept shouting. "Lift your head and fly!"

The warm wind raced straight up the side of the mountain, and so did he. Up! Going up! And, still, he flew, higher and higher.

Suddenly Arthur was above the edge of the cliff where he had jumped into the abyss. The Cloud People waved up at him, lifting their beautiful wings in a silent greeting.

"Isn't it beautiful?" Leela exclaimed.

"Oh yes! But how do I get down?"

"Tip your head like this," Leela said, demonstrating. In an instant she was swooping down, heading for the precipice where the Cloud People waited.

Arthur did as he was told. At the last possible moment, a gust of warm wind sent him spinning, head over heels. His blanket-wings got tangled up, and he closed his eyes, certain he was about to crash.

That's when the Cloud People joined their wings together and made a soft place for him to land. He bumped to a stop, a little bruised, but much to his amazement he was all in one piece.

Before he could stand up, Morf reached out a paw and shook his hand. "Let me be the first to congratulate you."

"Thanks," said Arthur, rising to his feet.

Before he could say anything else, the Cloud Master was there, helping him straighten out his blanket-wings. "We thank the wind that brought you back," he said. "We thank the sky for holding you up. We thank Leela, for showing you the way."

"It was nothing," Arthur said modestly.

"*Nothing* had nothing to do with it," the Cloud Master said. "You took the leap of faith and flew from the heart. Yours is a brave heart. From this moment forward, the Cloud People will know you as Courage. Arthur Courage."

"Courage!" the Cloud People sang. "Arthur Courage!"

And that's how the boy once known as Biscuit Butt got a brand-new name.

Now all he had to do was live up to it.

17

...

THE LUCKIEST
PERSON EVER
TO LIVE

FOR THE NEXT THREE days, Arthur practiced flying. With Leela showing the way, he learned the Six Ways of Soaring, and the Rising Flutter, and the Three Close Turns. The technique that gave him the most trouble was the Falling Dive, because the first part was plummeting straight down for at least a mile before you gradually opened your wings—not too fast or they'd tear off—and slowly, ever so slowly, pulled up.

"But what if I wait too long?" Arthur asked Leela before he tried it.

"That's easy. Don't."

"Don't? That's all you've got to say? Don't?" Arthur stood with his hands on his hips, glowering.

"The Falling Dive can't be explained," Leela said. "You learn by doing."

"Yes, but if I don't learn fast enough, I'll end up smashed like a bug on a windshield."

"What's a windshield?"

"Oh, never mind," Arthur said with a sigh. "Show me the Falling Dive."

He survived the Falling Dive—actually, it was great fun—and he practiced his Close Turns until he could do all three with his eyes closed. Amazing how easy it was to fly, once you got the hang of it.

Meanwhile Morf hung out on the very edge of the highest cliff, as comfortable as if he were perched on the side of his bed. "Nice turn, kid!" he would call out, encouraging Arthur. "Lovely flutter! I've never seen a better soar!" and so on. If Leela was the coach, Morf was the whole cheerleading squad.

Arthur was having so much fun that it was easy to forget why he'd been given the gift of flight in the first place. The truth is, he didn't want to think about Vydel's Mouth or the Nothing that was rising like a forgotten tide and would soon drown his Other Self.

When he did think about it, he felt less like Arthur Courage and more like Arthur-Scared-To-Death.

Once, while they were resting on a narrow cliff

beneath the clouds, Leela told him he was, in her opinion, the luckiest person ever to live.

"Really? Why is that? You mean because I learned to fly?"

"No, Arthur. Lots of people learn to fly. You're lucky because you've been given a chance to make a difference. If you succeed, you save REM World, and every other world, and all the stars in the sky. What could be more important than that?"

"Yeah," Arthur said morosely. "But if I fail, then I die, and everything disappears as if it never existed."

"See?" Leela exclaimed with delight. "You can't lose! If you fail, nobody knows because nobody exists!"

"I guess that's one way of looking at it."

"It's the only way," Leela assured him. "The answer is, don't fail."

"But suppose I manage to fly to Vydel's Mouth. What do I do when I get there?" The question had been plaguing him, and he was hoping the Cloud People knew the answer.

Leela shrugged. "You'll have to figure that out when the time comes."

"Isn't there a legend that explains what happens next?"

"Sorry, no. There's no legend. Because once you go through Vydel's Mouth, you can't come back."

"But *you* came back!"

"I flew above it," Leela said. "Not through it."

Arthur became very quiet. "What did you see? Besides the Nothing, I mean."

Leela's voice changed to a whisper. "Terrible things. Things out of my worst nightmares."

And she would speak no more of it.

. . .

Each evening the Cloud people gathered for the Ceremony of the Dying Sun. It was a beautiful ceremony—all those wings blossoming like huge flowers—but there was something sad about it, too—a kind of enchanting melancholy that made Arthur's heart ache, ever so slightly.

One evening—Arthur's fifth day in the World Above—the Cloud Master was especially formal and solemn. After the song faded with the setting of the sun, he asked Arthur to step forward and take his place in the inner circle, surrounded and protected by all the Cloud People.

When Arthur had done this, the Cloud Master raised his wings until the very tips pointed at the highest stars. "Let us give strength to Arthur Courage," he said. "He will take with him our strength and our love and our best wishes for the future."

"Strength!" the Cloud People sang. "Arthur Courage!"

Their wings touched his wings, and even though his wings had been made from a blanket, he felt it, anyway. A kind of electrical spark that made him feel warm on the inside, and maybe a little stronger, too.

"Thank you," he said. "Thank you for all you've done for me."

"We thank you, Arthur Courage, for what you are about to do," said the Cloud Master. "Now it is time for everyone to get some sleep. Tomorrow is a big day. The biggest day ever. Tomorrow is either the start of a new beginning, or the beginning of the end."

When Arthur finally got to sleep that night, his very last night with the Cloud People, he did not dream of clouds that tasted like pancakes. He dreamed of things that flew out of shadows.

Things with furious wings, and terrible, sharp talons.

18

. . .

INTO THE WILD
GREEN YONDER

THEY WERE AWAKENED an hour before dawn.

At first Arthur yawned and tried to roll over, but Morf reminded him that today was the day. There were promises to keep, and Arthur would be leaving a few moments after sunrise.

Arthur sat up as if he'd been jolted with electricity. "I wish it wasn't today," he said. "I wish it was tomorrow instead, or even yesterday." But he knew he was wishing for the impossible, and so he dragged himself from bed and put on his blanket-wings.

Leela and her father had been up for some time, making preparations.

"Your breakfast awaits," the Cloud Master announced with a smile.

On the steaming platter was a selection of food that Arthur never could have imagined. Cool melons cut out of rain clouds. Fluffy Sun flour waffles drenched in a dewdrop syrup. Bowls of porridge that glowed with the light of distant stars. Slices of toast so light, they floated above the plate, and plenty of moonberry jam.

"Eat up," the Cloud Master told him. "You're going to need all of your strength."

They ate until there was only one waffle left.

"You have it," said Leela.

"Oh, I couldn't," Arthur said.

"I insist," said Leela.

But it was too late. Morf polished it off, and he sat there licking the nearly invisible waffle crumbs and looking very pleased with himself.

"Time to go," the Cloud Master said, wrapping himself up in his wings.

. . .

The sunrise celebration was by now familiar to Arthur, and he sang along with the others, welcoming the dawn. He was beginning to feel very much at home in the World Above, and he hated to leave. But as Morf reminded him, a promise is a promise.

Leela took his hand, and they walked to the edge of the highest cliff. Far below, the clouds seemed to beckon, as if they knew that something very important was about to happen.

"What will you do?" Arthur asked Morf.

"What do you mean, 'What will I do?'" Morf looked startled. "I'm coming with you, of course."

And with that, Morf jumped up and tucked himself inside Arthur's shirt. His small, furry head poked out. "Ready when you are," he said, grinning. "Off we go into the wild green yonder!"

Arthur was flooded with relief. It was selfish, he knew, but he'd been sick at the thought of leaving Morf behind. Besides, he was terrified to face the ordeal of Vydel's Mouth alone.

It was Leela's mission to guide him as far below as she possibly dared. She took the responsibility very seriously. "Remember," she said, "wings out, head back. And let the wind do the work."

Together they stepped off the edge of the cliff and fell toward the World Below.

. . .

In the beginning, Arthur felt only exhilaration. The thrill of wind in his face.

The brilliant sun was warm on his back, and his blanket-wings thrummed with air.

It was glorious!

"This is the coolest," said Morf. His head poked out from under Arthur's chin.

They followed Leela, who was flying in great, slow

spirals. Gradually she glided down toward the thick layer of clouds. All around them, and far into the distance, mountain peaks emerged like steep, jagged islands in a fluffy white sea.

"Too bad we can't stay up here forever," said Morf. "Eat waffles for breakfast and then fly all day. What a life!"

Arthur sighed. He knew that nothing was forever, no matter how much you wanted it to be that way. And he was not looking forward to the challenge that lay ahead of him.

"The clouds look like they're made of cotton candy. Have you noticed?"

"They're not," Arthur told him, thinking about his experience with Leela.

A moment later they whooshed into the clouds. Instantly they lost sight of Leela; she had vanished into the mist. He could tell that Morf, nestled inside his shirt, was getting nervous. It was always a tense moment, entering a cloud, but a few seconds later they burst through, back into the pale green sky.

And there, right below them, Leela waited, pirouetting on her wings with the skill of a ballerina. Arthur knew he could practice for a hundred years, and he'd still never be able to fly so gracefully, and with such elegance.

It was like finding a living jewel waiting for him, right in the middle of the sky.

"You're doing fine!" she called out in an encouraging way.

"How much farther?"

They were above an immense canyon enclosed by high cliffs. The canyon was so deep, he couldn't see all the way to the bottom. Leela pointed down into the canyon and said, "Miles and miles to go. We've only just begun!"

Before Arthur could think of a reply, she tipped her wings and began a much steeper downward spiral. He followed as best as he could, but every once in a while, Leela would have to wait for him to catch up.

"Amazing," Morf said, piping up.

"Thanks."

"I didn't mean you, kid. I meant the girl."

Arthur would have blushed, but he was too busy trying to keep up. Or, rather, down. Because they were heading invariably and inevitably down. Down until they were below the high cliff walls that surrounded the deep canyon. Down until the sunlight gradually faded.

Down, down, down, into the zone of perpetual twilight.

Whereas their morning flight had begun gloriously, in the brightest of morning skies, they had now entered a kind of forever gloom. A not-quite-darkness that was more ominous and frightening than darkness itself.

"How much farther?" Arthur called out.

Even in the dimness he could make out the seriousness of Leela's expression. "I'm not sure," she said. "I'll know when we get there."

And so they kept spiraling down and down. Down through the pale, cool shadows.

Their wing tips almost brushed the canyon walls. Down for mile after mile, until they were so deep, the sky above was no longer visible.

Down, down, and then down some more.

As they swooped through the darkening shadows, Arthur felt a chill stealing over him. He wished he could wrap himself up in his blanket, but of course that was impossible. Fortunately Morf was warm and furry inside his shirt, and that helped a little.

Leela brushed lightly against him, getting his attention. "We're almost there," she whispered, as if the very shadows might hear her.

Arthur looked, but all he could see below him was darkness.

"You can just barely see the shape of it," she said. "Like a huge ring. Or an open mouth."

Vydel's Mouth. Yes, Arthur could just make it out. A ring of jagged, stony spires jutting up from the floor of the world. Spires that looked like a gigantic mouth bristling with razor-sharp fangs.

It was still more than a mile below them, but it filled Arthur with fear.

"Don't worry," Leela said. "You're supposed to be afraid."

"But your people gave me a new name! Arthur Courage. How can I be Arthur Courage if I'm afraid?"

"That's what courage is, Arthur. Doing something even though it frightens you."

Her words flooded him with warmth, and suddenly he knew what to do. It was the right and only thing. "You must go back, Leela," he told her. "Right now, while you can still find an updraft. That was the plan. Remember? You were just going to show me the way."

Leela hesitated.

"Go back!" he urged her. "Return to the World Above. Your people need you! You'll be the Cloud Master someday! Do it!"

Suddenly she swooped closer, and he felt her lips brush his cheek. "I'll miss you, Arthur Courage! Good luck! Save the world for me!"

And then she was gone, soaring upward through the darkening twilight. Arthur and Morf were alone, gliding down into the darkness.

Not too far below them, Vydel's Mouth seemed to beckon like death itself.

19

...

THE TERRIBLE
DARK TALONS

"So what's your plan?" Morf asked, poking his little head out and sniffing at the shadows that loomed below.

"I haven't got a plan."

"How can you save the universe if you haven't got a plan?"

How, indeed?

Arthur didn't have the faintest idea. Nobody seemed to know, not even the Cloud Master. The old legend said the visitor must go through Vydel's Mouth and find his way home. But how was Arthur supposed to do that? And what was he supposed to do when he got there?

At just that moment, when he was trying to think of a plan, Arthur caught sight of the Nothing. It was so dark here at the bottom of the world that he'd mistaken the Nothing for just another shadow.

But it wasn't just another shadow. It wasn't anything at all. That was the essence of the Nothing, of course—wherever it touched, nothing existed.

Impossible. And as Arthur stared in disbelief, he realized that the entire bottom of the canyon had ceased to exist.

The ring of jagged stone spires had so far kept the Nothing from flowing down into the cavernous area called Vydel's Mouth, but that wouldn't last much longer. Once the Nothing had filled the bottom of the canyon—or emptied it, depending on your point of view—it would spill over the top of the spires. Vydel's Mouth would cease to exist, and with it, Arthur's chance of finding his way home.

Arthur was just about to begin his final descent when suddenly the air was split by a terrifying noise.

CAWWWWW! CAWWWWW! CAWWWWW!

Huge crowlike birds poured up out of Vydel's Mouth, rising like black smoke. They headed right for Arthur and Morf.

CAWWWWW! CAWWWWW! CAWWWWW!

The mob of crows beat the air with black shiny

wings, and there was nothing Arthur could do to stop them. Nor could he get away—he simply couldn't fly as fast as a bird. All he could do was glide on his blanket-wings, and the glide path carried him right into the midst of the attacking crows.

CAWWWWW! CAWWWWW! CAWWWWW!

The air was thick with black, beating wings. Sharp, snipping beaks and terrible dark talons began to tear at his blanket-wings.

"Get away!" Arthur shouted. "Leave us alone!" But the crows weren't the least bit frightened.

One of the shrieking birds landed on Arthur's head and began to pull his hair. Others hovered just above, using their talons to shred his wings. Fortunately the blanket was very strong, and the crows were obviously frustrated. They cawed and screeched and poked at him until Arthur wanted to scream like a crow—and he did.

"CAWWWWW!" he screeched. "CAWWWWWW!"

That was when one of the attacking crows tore open Arthur's shirt.

The shirt where Morf was hiding.

"Noooooooooo!" Morf plunged through the air, heading straight for the sharpest spire of stone.

. . .

Morf was plummeting to his doom, and there was nothing Arthur could do about it. He was so horrified, he could barely feel the crows tearing at his wings. His little friend was going to die, and it was all his fault. He never should have let Morf come along.

"Morf!" Arthur cried. "I wish there was something I could do! I wish it was me instead of you!"

And at just that moment he remembered something Grog had said when he left them on the mountain.

"If you get in trouble, ask Morf to change, and he will."

At that time, Arthur had been puzzled, but with all the excitement of meeting the Cloud People, there hadn't been room in his mind for figuring out what Grog had meant. He had even less time now, but it didn't matter, because they were in really big trouble, and there was nothing else he *could* do except yell: "Change, Morf! Please change!" He yelled as loud as he could and hoped for the best.

At first, nothing happened. Morf continued to fall head over heels, getting smaller and smaller.

And then, all at once, it happened. Morf changed. The little creature with the big furry tail morphed into a bird, swooping up and away just before he struck the rocks.

Arthur was so astonished, he wasn't aware that the crows had almost shredded his wings to pieces. He concentrated on watching the bird that had once been Morf, or was still Morf in a different form—he didn't know which.

The bird was almost the same size as Morf had been

before the change. Which meant he was only slightly larger than the attacking crows, and he was outnumbered by the hundreds. But the Morf-bird showed no fear, and it headed straight for Arthur as fast as it could fly.

The crows were frightened of the strange new bird—they were scared of anything that wasn't afraid of them—and they swarmed away, shrieking and cawing.

As the new bird got closer, Arthur saw that it had Morf's face.

"Hurry!" Morf urged him. "Those wings won't last much longer, and I'm too small to save you!"

That's when Arthur realized that his blanket-wings had begun to disintegrate. The blanket flapped and tore. Little pieces of it were carried away by the cold wind that seemed to be sucking him down, right into the center of Vydel's Mouth. Arthur had no choice: He had to go down as fast as he could, avoiding the sharp stone teeth, heading for the impenetrable darkness.

Down he went, faster and faster, leaving bits of his wings behind. Morf stayed with him, shouting encouragement. "That's it, kid! You're doing fine! Don't give up now, we're almost there!"

Yes, but where was *there*? It was so dark, and the cold wind made Arthur's eyes water. He couldn't really see beyond the tips of his disintegrating wings.

"Hang on!" cried Morf, beating his own little wings to slow down.

But it was too late. The last piece of blanket ripped away. Arthur ceased flying and began to fall.

The darkness came at him like a huge fist.

"Look out!" cried Morf.

The last thing Arthur remembered was smashing belly-first into the giant rocks at the very bottom of Vydel's Mouth.

20

...

THE SCRABBLING
OF CLAWS

HE WOKE UP IN the dark.

"Am I dead?" he groaned.

"Not yet," said a familiar voice.

It was Morf, who had returned to his form as a creature with four paws and a big furry tail. He'd been flicking his tail at Arthur's nose, trying to wake him.

"What happened?" Arthur asked. He tried to sit up, but everything hurt.

"It wasn't the falling," said Morf. "It was the sudden stop."

"Oh!" And Arthur remembered slamming stomach-first into the unforgiving rocks. "Where are we?" As his eyes adjusted, he was able to see a little.

"We're in a bad place, kid," said Morf, keeping his voice low. "And we're not alone."

"What!" Arthur looked around, but he could barely make out his surroundings. Rocks and more rocks. Big rocks, small rocks, and in-between rocks. Darkness and rocks, that's all there seemed to be at the bottom of the world.

"Ssssh," Morf cautioned. "They'll hear us."

"Who will hear us?" Arthur whispered.

"Them," said Morf, very quietly.

Arthur decided to shut up and listen. And that's when he heard it. A distant moaning that could have been the wind, but wasn't. And another, closer, more frightening sound: the scrabbling of claws on a hard surface.

Cautiously, Arthur sat up. He had to stifle his groans because he'd been badly bruised by his collision with the rocks. His stomach felt as if it had been punched, and his nose was swollen. His hands ached, like he'd been catching baseballs without a glove.

Scrabble, scrabble.

Whatever it was, it was getting closer.

"What do we do?" Arthur whispered.

"Try not to be too appetizing."

Now that Arthur thought about it, the scrabble of claws was a hungry sort of noise. He decided that the best thing to do was remain very still and quiet. Maybe whatever was making the hungry, scratching noise would go away and leave them alone.

When he was little, he'd tried the same technique on the spooky things that lived under his bed. It had worked, but the under-the-bed things weren't real. Whatever was making this noise was very real indeed.

"Hold your breath," Morf suggested in a voice so small, Arthur could barely hear him.

Arthur held his breath. The scrabbling claws surrounded the rock where he and Morf were sitting. He kept his eyes squeezed shut because he couldn't bear to look. Anything that made a noise like that had to be too horrible to contemplate.

Scrabble, scrabble.

Much closer. Close enough to touch.

Arthur hugged himself. The last thing he wanted to do was touch the thing making the claw-scrabble noise. So he didn't touch anything. But something touched him. Something cool and leathery. Something that was definitely not human.

Peep, peep.

It sounded like a newly hatched bird, only much, much louder. Arthur was so frightened, his heart felt like a chunk of melting ice. But he opened his eyes, anyhow. And there, staring right at him, was an eye almost as big as his head.

"Ahhh!" he yelled.

The eye blinked.

Perched on the rock was a creature that looked like a giant brown soccer ball with stubby leather wings and two big eyes. Added to that were a pair of very clumsy feet with overgrown claws, and a curved beak that looked like an upside-down smile.

"Borons," Morf said, breathing a sigh of relief. "They're harmless at this age, I think."

"At this age?" Arthur asked. He was thinking that the goofy-looking, leather-bird creatures were sort of cute, in a strange, space-alien way.

"They've obviously just hatched," Morf explained. "Grown up, they can be quite vicious."

Just as he said that, the rock they were sitting on moved. Morf and Arthur scrambled off. The clumsy-looking creature used its upside-down beak to peck at the rock.

At first Arthur was puzzled, but then he realized that the rock wasn't a rock at all. It was an egg. With a little help from the weird-looking creature Morf called a boron, the eggshell cracked open, and another leathery, birdlike creature emerged.

"Why do they call them borons?" Arthur wanted to know.

"Because they're not very bright," Morf explained. "Bird moron, hence the name *boron*."

Arthur soon realized that most of the "rocks" around them were actually boron eggs. They began to hatch, one after another, and sometimes two or three at once. In a very short time the dark, cavernous area was teeming with them.

And Morf was right. The borons weren't particularly intelligent. In fact, they were downright stupid. They kept bumping into each other and falling down. Some of them got their big, goofy-looking claws entwined, like shoelaces tied together, and just sat there staring as if feet were much too complicated to understand. Others tried to peck open rocks—actual rocks, not eggs—and when they became frustrated, they fell down.

"Borons fall down all the time," Morf explained. "They're famous for it."

"At least they're not trying to eat us," said Arthur.

"Not yet." Morf sighed and began grooming his tail.

Arthur suddenly remembered how Morf had avoided crashing by turning into a bird. "Why didn't you tell me you could do that?" he asked petulantly. "Change into a bird, I mean."

"I assumed you knew," Morf said matter-of-factly. "I'm sure it was in the instructions."

"Oh, bother the instructions," said Arthur.

"All morfs can change shape, upon request," Morf explained. "It's in our nature."

"You mean there's more than one of you?"

"There's only one of me. But there are other morfs, of course."

"I had no idea!"

"If you'd read the instructions—"

"Enough!" said Arthur. Just then a boron stumbled over and pecked at the back of his head.

"Ow!" cried Arthur, and the surprised boron fell down.

Peep, peep, it said, sounding confused. *Peep, peep.*

"Peep, peep, yourself," said Arthur, rubbing the sore spot on the back of his head.

"May I make a suggestion?" Morf asked casually. "We ought to move along, before their mother returns to the nest. I'd like to avoid contact with an adult boron, if at all possible."

"Mother?" Arthur said. "Nest?"

Before Morf could respond, the ground beneath them began to shake.

"Oops," said Morf. "I'm afraid we're too late."

21

...

THE TROUBLE
WITH BORONS

THE NEWLY HATCHED borons didn't know what to do, so they stampeded.

"Look out!" Arthur cried as one of them bounced off a rock and nearly crushed Morf.

Morf dusted himself off and gave Arthur a sharp look of disapproval. "Any suggestions?" he asked.

"I was hoping you had an idea." As Arthur spoke, he ducked to his left, narrowly avoiding a boron that was rolling by like a bowling ball.

Meanwhile the ground continued to shake as the mother boron came closer.

"I'm fresh out of ideas," Morf said stubbornly.

"You're the one who's saving the universe. How about saving us, for starters?"

Just then two borons collided and fell to the ground, so dazed, they could hardly move.

That gave Arthur an idea. "Grab hold!" he cried, and he leaped on one of the befuddled borons as if it were a horse.

Morf shook his head fretfully, but he climbed onto the back of the other boron. There were no saddles, of course, and it's not easy to perch on top of a giant soccer ball, but Arthur grabbed hold of the stubby leather wings and held on tight as the boron came back to life. "Here we go!" he cried, and sure enough, the borons were off and running, back in the stampede.

The hatchlings were all racing for the darkest part of the cavern. They were heading for the thundering approach of something very large indeed. It was all Arthur and Morf could do to hang on. They tried to steer by grabbing the stubby wings, but it was no use. No matter what they did, the stampede was carrying them directly into danger.

Before long, Arthur realized he'd been wrong about heading for the darkest part of the cavern. As they got closer, he saw that the huge dark patch was actually a giant creature—the mother boron. She was stamping her tremendous claws, causing the ground to shake. When she flapped her immense wings, dozens of little borons spun like leaves in the wind.

Arthur crouched as low as he could, praying the huge beast wouldn't spot him in the dim light. Suddenly they were in the worst place possible: right under the mother boron. Her great clawed feet came slashing down. Each of the claws were as big around as Arthur, and he came two inches from being crushed.

The first claw missed him, but the borons they were riding fell down in confusion, and Arthur quickly rolled along the ground, avoiding the other claw. It just missed him, and then he was up and running.

He looked down and saw Morf beside him, keeping up as if it were no effort at all. "We made it! What's next?"

"Keep going!"

And so they ran into the darkness for as long and as hard as they could. By the time Arthur had to stop and catch his breath, the stampeding borons were far behind them.

"I wish I had a flashlight," Arthur lamented. It was very, very dark. "I don't suppose you know where we are?"

"Haven't got a clue," said Morf. "Obviously, we're underground."

"Obviously."

Arthur decided to explore by putting his hands out, and cautiously he walked from side to side. After bumping into a couple of hard surfaces, he could tell that they were in some sort of large tunnel.

"Well," he said. "We can't go back to the boron nest. So there's really only one direction left."

"Forward?" asked Morf.

"Forward," said Arthur, leading the way.

They walked in the dark tunnel for a very long time.

. . .

After many hours of trudging along, Arthur detected a faint light far, far ahead of them. He and Morf hurried toward it.

At first the faint light seemed to recede as they approached, so that it never got any closer. This was frustrating, and Arthur concluded it must be a mirage of some kind.

"Ridiculous," scoffed Morf. "Mirages don't happen underground."

"Yeah? How do you know?" Arthur asked. He was tired and hungry, and that put him in an argumentative mood.

"It's just something I know," said Morf evasively.

"Well," sniffed Arthur, "I think *you're* the one who's being ridiculous."

"Double the same to you," said Morf.

"Oh, yeah?" said Arthur. "Maybe I'll ask you to change into a glazed doughnut, and then I'll eat you in three bites."

Morf stopped in his tracks and folded his little arms. "I demand an apology."

Arthur ignored him. "Follow me," he finally said. "I think the light is getting closer."

Morf stood his ground.

"Oh, all right," Arthur said. "I apologize. Can we go now?"

Morf began walking again. "Just for your information," he said, "I can't morph into an inanimate object."

"I wouldn't have asked you to do that, really," Arthur said, and he meant it. Still, the thought of a glazed doughnut made his stomach feel incredibly empty. To take his mind off being hungry, he decided to ask Morf a question that had been nagging at him. "We came through the place called Vydel's Mouth, right? So who is Vydel?"

Morf was shocked. "You flew into Vydel's Mouth without knowing?"

Arthur shrugged. "I never thought to ask."

Morf shook his head in wonder. "Vydel is a demon. He's the Demon of all Demons, and Lord of the World Below. Legends say that he has three heads, and each one is uglier than the next."

"Legends?" Arthur asked. "You mean he's not real?"

"No one knows," Morf said. "Maybe we'll find out."

"I hope not."

When Arthur looked up, the light ahead was no longer faint, and it was much, much closer. Strangely enough, the light seemed to be making a noise.

It sounded very much like water.

22

...

THE RIVER UNDER
THE WORLD

THE SOUND OF water grew louder and louder, until it was a roaring river. And that is exactly what Arthur and Morf discovered when at last they came to the end of the tunnel.

The light they'd seen was the river itself, for the water glowed, as if the river and sunlight somehow had been combined. And yet there was no sun, not this far under the world.

"Weird," Arthur said as they stared at the river, which flowed off into the darkness like a glowing ribbon of light. It was strange, yes, and somehow wonderful, too.

"This must be the River Under the World," Morf said, sounding more than a little amazed. "I always thought it was just another legend."

The water was fast-moving, and each eddy and swirl glowed brightly. The River Under the World was wide—so wide, they couldn't see to the other side.

"I suppose you could change into a fish and swim across," Arthur said, "but I can't. Any ideas?"

Before Morf could think of an answer, a voice came out of the water. "Pay the toll," it said.

Arthur jumped back, startled. Was it possible that the river itself was talking?

The voice spoke again. "Pay the toll," it said, quite peevishly. "Pay the toll, and you can ride to the end of the river, or to the end of the world, whichever comes first."

Working up his courage, Arthur peered over the edge of the riverbank. There, just below him, a strange-looking old man was immersed up to his neck in the glowing water.

"Who are you?" Arthur asked.

The old man stared at him as if trying to decide whether he intended to answer. "I'm Mr. Pockets," he finally said. "Not that it's any of your business."

"What are you doing in the water?" Arthur asked.

"Isn't it obvious?" the old man said grouchily. "I'm fishing."

Grumbling to himself, Mr. Pockets climbed out of

the water and onto the riverbank. His many pockets were full of wriggling fish. As the water dripped away, the old man removed a small fish from one of his pockets, examined it briefly, popped it into his mouth, and swallowed the fish in one gulp. "What are you staring at?" Mr. Pockets frowned at Arthur. "You'd think the boy never saw anyone fishing, staring like that."

Arthur was so astonished that he couldn't think of anything to say.

"I'm the Official Toll Keeper for the River Under the World," said Mr. Pockets with great dignity. "If you wish to cross the river, you will have to pay the toll."

"This is rotten luck," Arthur muttered. "I don't have any money. Do you have any money, Morf?"

Morf shook his head.

"Money?" said Mr. Pockets. "Did I say anything about money?"

"But you said we had to pay the toll," Arthur said, confused.

"Toll, yes. But payment can be in any of several forms." Mr. Pockets spoke as if reciting from a rule book. "A payment is a transaction, meaning that you, the Customer, give me, the Official Toll Keeper, something of value. Which could be almost anything," he added.

The only thing that Arthur had that might be remotely valuable was the mysterious wristwatch loaned to him by Galump, and there was no way he could give that away, not for anything.

"But I don't have anything of value," he said helplessly. "Not that I can trade."

"Absolute nonsense," Mr. Pockets said. He harrumphed in disgust. "Everyone has something of value. Think. What do you have that I do not?"

While he waited for an answer, the Toll Keeper absentmindedly reached into his pockets and munched on a few fish. It was very disconcerting for Arthur to try to talk with a man who had a small fishtail poking out of the corner of his mouth.

What do I have that Mr. Pockets does not? Arthur racked his brains but couldn't think of a thing.

"Well? What do you have that I do not?" Mr. Pockets repeated.

"No idea," Arthur finally said, feeling defeated.

"No? Absolutely none? You haven't even got *one* idea? Because," he hinted, "an idea is something of value." As he waited for a reply, Mr. Pockets made urgent signals with his hands, indicating that he was giving clues to Arthur, and he expected the boy to make the most of it.

"Oh!" said Arthur. "I get it! You mean I can tell you an idea, and that will pay the toll."

"Not just *any* idea," Mr. Pockets stressed. "An idea of value. An idea that is worth something to me in particular. Something I need to know."

Arthur thought, and he thought. He had a number of interesting ideas, many of which involved food. For instance, since milk and cookies tasted so good, why not make a cookie-flavored milk? Instead of chocolate milk, you'd have cookie milk. Use that idea and you'd become a millionaire for sure. But somehow he didn't think Mr. Pockets would be interested. He was after something else.

And that's when Arthur had an idea about an idea, which is in itself a rare and valuable occurrence.

"I know something that's very important," he said triumphantly. "Something you need to know."

"Excellent! Wonderful!" cried Mr. Pockets. "Tell me, please!"

"Here goes," said Arthur, clearing his throat. "Unless I find my way home, and somehow stop the Nothing from rising, the entire universe will come to an end."

In the silence that followed, Mr. Pockets's eyes seemed about to bug out of his head. Finally he exclaimed, "Extraordinary! That's the most profound and powerful idea I've ever heard. Is it true, by any chance?"

"I'm afraid so."

"Dear me," said Mr. Pockets. Absentmindedly he began to take wriggling fish from his pockets. He dropped them gently back into the river. "This is really quite exceptional. I was expecting an idea like

'Brush your teeth, or you'll get cavities,' and here you've given me news that the universe may soon be ending. How did it happen?"

Arthur explained as much as he could of his unexpected journey to REM World. How because he hadn't read the instructions and forgot to bring his helmet he was in two places at once, which was impossible but nevertheless true, and that's how the Nothing had found a way through a crack into the universe, and if Arthur didn't get back to his basement and stop it somehow, before long Everything would be Nothing.

"And you say the Cloud People advised you to go through Vydel's Mouth to find your way home?"

"Yes. But all we had to go on was some old legend."

"Hmmm," said Mr. Pockets. "Legends can be useful. A legend is just an idea with a story attached, you know. In this case, they almost had it right. 'Through Vydel's Mouth' is simply a variation on 'From Vydel's Mouth.'"

"What do you mean?" Arthur asked in alarm.

"I mean if you want to know how to find your way home, you should ask Vydel himself."

"But the legends say Vydel is a demon!"

Mr. Pockets rolled his eyes. "I didn't say Vydel was a nice person, did I? As a matter of fact, he's not a person at all. He's a great many things, and one of them is a very bad and evil demon. But the point is, Vydel knows almost everything there is to know. And you're allowed to ask him one question. If he considers your question interesting, he'll answer."

"What if he doesn't consider the question interesting?"

Mr. Pockets shrugged. "Then you're dead," he said. "Or worse."

"What could be worse than dead?" Arthur asked hesitantly.

"Believe me," said Mr. Pockets, "that's something you really *don't* want to know."

23

. . .

WHY THE RIVER
GLOWED

"YOU'D BETTER BE on your way," Mr. Pockets advised. "I'll provide my finest conveyance."

"Conveyance?" asked Arthur, who had never heard the word before.

"A means of getting from here to there," said Mr. Pockets. "In this case, a rather splendid raft."

The raft looked anything but splendid. It consisted of a pair of logs strapped on either side of two upright barrels. The tops were cut off from the barrels so that the passengers stood inside them, which meant if you were Arthur's size, your head and shoulders were barely above the surface of the water.

"The river goes to the end of the world and beyond," Mr. Pockets explained, once he had Arthur and Morf situated in the barrel raft. "I've never actually been that far myself, but I've heard some interesting tales about what you'll find when you get there."

"Um, what sort of tales?" Arthur asked with concern.

"Best you discover that on your own," said Mr. Pockets. "All I know for sure is that you'll find Vydel in the place called Beyond."

"I'm not sure I want to meet this Vydel demon, or whatever he is," said Arthur. "He sounds frightening and terrible."

But the raft was already moving into the current, and Mr. Pockets was standing on the riverbank waving farewell. "Best of luck, Arthur Courage!" he called out. "You'll need it!"

"How do you think he knew my name?" Arthur asked Morf, who was sitting on the rim of his barrel.

"Maybe he found it in one of his pockets," Morf said, and then he began grooming his tail as if he didn't have a care in the world.

Arthur didn't have time to ponder the mystery of how Mr. Pockets knew he'd been named Courage, because the raft was gaining speed, sweeping them out into the middle of the glowing waters.

The river flowed through a gigantic cavern, and the light from the water illuminated it. Stalactites loomed from above like huge icicles frozen in stone. The effect was beautiful, in a frightening sort of way, because Arthur knew that if a stalactite broke loose, it would probably sink their little raft.

"I wonder how long it will take to get there," he said, for he was very anxious about Vydel and wanted to be done with the journey.

"That's easy," Morf piped up. "It will take exactly as long as it takes, and not a moment more."

"You're no help."

"I'm too busy worrying to be helpful," said Morf, although, as usual, he didn't look remotely worried or concerned.

"What are you worried about?"

"Are you kidding? What am I *not* worried about?" Morf shrugged. "Okay, for starters, I'm worried about why the river glows. There has to be a reason, and I'll bet it isn't a good one."

. . .

The answer came an hour or so later, and by that time Arthur had fallen asleep, lulled by the rush of the water and the gentle bobbing of the barrel raft.

"Uh-oh," said Morf, and that was enough to bring Arthur instantly awake.

Directly ahead of them, a glowing fin had appeared on the surface. Almost immediately after, another fin appeared directly behind it, and then another and another.

"S-s-sharks," said Arthur in a voice so small, it could barely be heard.

But they were not shark fins, as they soon discovered, because a huge head lifted from the water. Connected to the head was a very long neck, and it soon became apparent that all of the fins belonged to the same animal, and they ran along its back like plates of armor.

It was a kind of giant river serpent, and it glowed so brightly that it made the whole river shine with eerie light. Or rather it was one of a number of glowing river serpents, because a series of heads soon lifted from the water until the raft was surrounded on all sides by the silent and mysterious creatures.

"What do we do now?" Arthur whispered, loud enough for Morf to hear.

"There's nothing we *can* do," said Morf. "Besides, I'm not sure they mean us any harm."

Indeed, the river serpents seemed to be carefully avoiding the raft, as if they knew their undulating tails might be dangerous to a craft so small and fragile. The serpents swam in magnificent silence, as if escorting the little raft was their solemn duty.

Which, as it turned out, was exactly what they were doing.

"Maybe they know why you're here," Morf suggested.

"How would they know that?"

"It could be they were listening when you told Mr. Pockets about the Nothing."

It was a reasonable explanation, but Arthur was never to know for sure because the serpents did not speak. They formed a silent convoy, accompanying the raft but keeping a respectful distance, and their gleaming bodies were so bright, it was like being surrounded by sinuous pillars of daylight.

If there were any other creatures in the river—creatures who might threaten the little barrel raft—they were obviously not willing to risk swimming among the huge sea serpents.

"We should have asked Mr. Pockets for some food," Arthur said as they drifted along. "I'm so hungry, I'd almost be willing to eat a fish."

"Maybe Vydel will invite us to supper," said Morf.

"Maybe he'll *have* us for supper," Arthur replied.

The prospect of being eaten was once again such a real possibility that neither of them spoke for some time. Meanwhile the raft continued to flow with the river, surrounded by the glowing serpents, and gradually the dark, foreboding landscape of the eerie underground cavern began to change.

The River Under the World became narrower, and faster. The raft picked up speed. The waters became choppy, and soon the barrel raft was bobbing violently.

"Hang on!" Arthur cried. "Rapids!"

"It's rapid, all right," Morf said, clinging to his barrel.

Arthur was less fearful when he realized that the river serpents were protecting them from the worst parts of the rapids. They guided the raft through swirls and currents and helped the raft avoid the large, pointed rocks that reared up like miniature islands.

He wondered, not for the first time, if Mr. Pockets had somehow asked the serpents to look out for them. Maybe it was all part of his "splendid conveyance." Or maybe the glowing serpents really had overheard the talk about the Nothing and decided to help, as Morf had suggested. Whatever, if the huge creatures hadn't been there to help, Arthur and Morf surely would have drowned.

It was there, right in the midst of the perilous rapids, that Arthur realized something quite profound, and indeed something that would soon prove very useful. What he realized was this: Everything alive was part of the Everything. And therefore everything alive had a very good reason to want to help him defeat the Nothing. Morf, the Frog People, Grog the Giant, the Cloud People, Mr. Pockets, the sea serpents—they all wanted him to succeed.

Everybody on REM World was rooting for him.

And that's when Arthur started to believe that, with the help of others, he might actually be able to save the universe.

"Hey!" Morf was saying, trying to get his attention. "Do you hear that?"

"Hear what?" asked Arthur, still basking in the comforting idea that he might actually survive.

"Listen!"

Arthur listened. And then he heard it. A sigh so large, and so loud, that it filled the air. It sounded like a stadium full of cheering people, but it wasn't.

It was a waterfall. An enormous waterfall. And they were about to tumble over it and fall into the abyss below.

24

. . .

TO THE END
OF THE WORLD
AND BEYOND

AHEAD OF THEM the rapids vanished into a cloud of mist created by the great waterfall, and the sigh became a roar as they were swept closer and closer to the edge.

"We don't even have a paddle!" Arthur shouted.

He pawed at the water with his hands, but it was no use. They were going much too fast to slow down. He was about to shout at Morf to change into a bird and save himself, when suddenly a serpent's giant head appeared right next to the barrel raft.

Carefully the serpent nudged the raft, pushing it toward the riverbank. Another serpent joined in the effort, and within a few moments the raft was bumping up against the shore.

Arthur and Morf scrambled out and hugged the dry ground as the raft was swept away.

"They saved us," Arthur gasped, but when he turned around to thank them, the river serpents were gone. All he could see was their eerie glow retreating slowly into the mist.

"I've had enough of boats and rafts," Morf said, shaking water from his fur. "Let's stick to dry land from now on."

"We didn't have a choice, did we?"

"Oh, never mind." Morf looked around. "So, here we are at the end of the world. It doesn't look like much."

It didn't look like much because there wasn't much to see. Just white mist rising from the falls, which were so close that the sound of cascading water made the air tremble.

"We have to get to the place called Beyond," Arthur reminded Morf.

Carefully Arthur made his way along the riverbank to the edge of the waterfall. It was difficult to see through the thick, wet mist, but the falls went over a very steep cliff and plunged so far down that Arthur couldn't make out the bottom. "Somehow we have to get down there."

"Looks impossible." Morf's whiskers were glistening with waterfall dew.

"Yes, but it can't be impossible. There has to be a way. We can't give up now."

This was very unlike Arthur. He'd had plenty of practice in giving up. Faced with a daunting task in class or gym, he'd said to himself, *Why bother?* But the "why bother" option didn't exist in REM World. If Arthur gave up, the Nothing would keep rising, and when the last star faded from the sky, it would be Arthur's fault.

"I wonder what's behind the waterfall?" Arthur rubbed his damp chin thoughtfully.

"Behind the waterfall?" asked Morf. "Who ever heard of anything behind a waterfall?"

"We won't know until we look."

Very carefully Arthur edged his way over the cliff, blindly feeling for a foothold. Almost immediately his foot encountered something solid.

"Steps!" he said. "It feels like a stairway of some kind."

"How very odd," said Morf, sounding puzzled. "Do you think it's safe?"

"Nothing is safe. But we don't really have any other choice, do we?"

When they had both worked their way over the edge, they could make out steps carved into the wet stone. The ancient stairway curved steeply down, disappearing into the veil of mist behind the falls.

"We're sure to get wet," Morf grumbled. "And I *hate* to get wet."

"Don't be a doofus," Arthur said. He inched his way down the slippery steps.

"What's a doofus?"

"No time to explain. Hurry up! And be careful."

"Now there's a contradiction in terms," Morf muttered to himself. But he hopped from step to step, following Arthur's lead.

Soon the falls were thundering overhead, close enough for Arthur to reach out and touch. The steady stream of water had a hypnotic effect, and Arthur found he had to look away or it would make him dizzy. And dizzy is the last thing you want to be when you're going down a slippery stone stairway behind an immense and powerful waterfall.

There was barely enough room for them to make their way down, step by careful step. Lean out too far, and the powerful waterfall would snatch them. Hugging the face of the cliff, Arthur slowly descended. Soon he was soaked, for the mist was as thick as rain, although wonderfully warm.

"I think these stairs go down forever," Morf complained. "I'm completely wet, in case you hadn't noticed."

"I noticed. It can't be much farther."

But it was much farther. They continued down the narrow stone steps for what seemed like hours, never more than a few feet from the inside of the cascading water, which burbled and sighed like a living thing. Every muscle in Arthur's body ached.

Then a strange and beautiful thing happened. Gradually it began to get lighter. Sunlight came through the waterfall, and Arthur thought he recognized the pale green of the sky, although he couldn't be sure. But the prospect of eventually emerging into the light of day kept his spirits up, and it filled his heart with joy. Which was the strangest thing of all, because he knew that he was getting closer and closer to the place where the demon Vydel lived, and that was not a happy thought—not at all.

Finally the ancient stairway ended, and they found themselves on a narrow stone path that veered out from under the falls.

"Come on!" cried Arthur. "We're almost there!"

Indeed they were. Within a few minutes they were clear of the falls, and Arthur found himself blinded by the brightness of the sky.

When his eyes adjusted, Arthur saw that they were in a lush garden. Giant ferns glittered with waterfall dew, and the smell was so clean and fresh, he drank in the air, filling his lungs.

"I've heard of this place," Morf said quietly. "It's called the Demon's Garden. The legends say anyone who enters here is lost, and will never be seen again."

"Forget those rotten old legends," Arthur told him. "It's lovely. And why would a demon have a garden, anyhow?"

But Morf was too busy shaking himself dry to respond.

"Look," said Arthur. "The path goes on."

As a matter of fact, the path did go on and on, curving here and there among the giant ferns and plants. The vegetation was like nothing Arthur had ever seen on Earth, not that he'd ever paid much attention to plants and flowers. Most of the blossoms were huge—bigger than pumpkins—and the fragrance was such that he no longer felt hungry, as if the air itself were good enough to eat.

They stopped to rest, and with a sigh Morf plopped down on a huge blue leaf. "Do you mind if I take a short nap?" he asked. "I'm exhausted."

Without waiting for a reply, Morf curled up and purred himself to sleep. Arthur yawned—he wasn't tired at all, so why was he yawning?—and in less than a minute, he, too, was fast asleep.

He slept so soundly that he didn't hear the leaves begin to rustle, nor was he aware that they were not alone.

25

INTRUDERS IN THE GARDEN

T HE BUZZ WOKE HIM.

BZZZZZ. BZZZZZZ.

It sounded like a small airplane diving out of the pale green sky. The first thing Arthur did was slap at his ear, thinking that a mosquito was trapped there, and that's why it sounded so loud.

But it wasn't a mosquito. It was a bee. A huge bee. A bee the size of a small, flying attack dog. And it was circling over them in tight, furious circles, zooming so close that Arthur could feel its wings brushing against the top of his head.

"Help!" Arthur cried, trying to shield himself. "Help!"

He ran, crashing through dense foliage, desperate to get away. Arthur wasn't fond of normal, everyday bees. A giant bee was enough to make his heart thud like an unbalanced washing machine.

BZZZZZZZ! BZZZZZZZZZ!

The huge bee seemed to be furious with the frightened boy, and it didn't help that in Arthur's haste to get away he'd smashed up some of the giant flower blossoms.

·Morf had managed to hide himself under a large leaf. "Don't move! Try to be still!"

"A giant bee is attacking me!" Arthur cried out. "How can you expect me to keep still?"

He continued to thrash through the dense foliage, trying to get away. But it was no use. Wherever he went, the giant bee followed. As Arthur trampled more and more flowers, the bee became more and more enraged.

Finally it stopped chasing him and began to execute an elaborate series of figure eights in the air above Arthur's head.

"Oh no," said Morf. "It's signaling for reinforcements."

"You mean there's more than one of these things?"

"I'm afraid so."

Almost immediately they heard the leaf-shaking drone of an approaching squadron of giant bees. The sky grew dark with angry insects. They dove and swooped, brandishing foot-long stingers, narrowly missing Arthur. He covered his head with his hands and tried to burrow into the foliage, but it was no use. No matter what he did, he couldn't escape the bees.

Five or six of them worked together, using their stingers to slash the leaves just above his head. In another moment, he'd have no protection at all.

"Morf, change!" Arthur cried. "Fly away and save yourself!"

He cowered beneath the last leaf, waiting for the stingers to stab him to death. The droning noise changed, and suddenly something landed on his shoulder. Writhing in horror, Arthur looked up to see a giant bee.

The bee had Morf's face.

Arthur was astonished. He'd expected Morf to change into a bird, not one of the deadly bees.

"Don't worry," said Morf, his voice buzzing strangely. "I've got a plan."

And with that, he left Arthur's shoulder and began to fly a series of elaborate loop-the-loops. The other bees stopped attacking and hovered. They watched Morf, who was using bee signals to communicate.

"NO DANGER," he spelled out. "IGNORANT VISITOR MEANS NO HARM."

The squadron of bees separated and flew to individual flower blossoms, as if waiting to see what would happen next.

"Stand up slowly," Morf buzzed. "Tell them you're sorry you disturbed their flowers."

Arthur did as he was told. Apparently the bees

understood, because after buzzing busily among themselves, and constructing all sorts of elaborate signals, the bees seemed to have arrived at a decision.

"Great," buzzed Morf. "They've accepted your apology."

One by one, the bees lifted from their blossoms and slowly flew off.

"They want us to follow them," said Morf in his regular voice.

Between blinks of an eye, he'd changed back to his normal Morf-like self.

"Follow them where?" asked Arthur with some trepidation.

Morf shrugged. "Bee language isn't all that specific," he said. "All I know for sure is that they've been awaiting an important visitor. And they've decided it must be you."

The bees kept a respectful distance, hovering almost but not quite out of sight. Meanwhile Arthur and Morf continued along the winding path. Eventually they passed out of the flower garden and entered a dense, junglelike forest.

"Do they have tigers in REM World?" Arthur whispered. This appeared to be an ideal place for them.

"Tigers? Hmmm. Nothing by that name."

"Good," said Arthur. He was somewhat relieved. Although the forest was very, very thick. And dark. And dangerous.

"No tigers. But of course there are many other savage beasts," Morf said, musing. "Ripons, for instance. And greeps. And don't forget zargas. A zarga will tear you to pieces in an instant. Zargas live in trees and drop down when you least expect it." He looked up at the thick tree branches.

"Do you see one?" Arthur whispered anxiously.

"I'm not sure," Morf said, squinting. "Probably not. Luckily, zargas hate bees."

Arthur was grateful. The buzzy drone of rapidly moving wings was suddenly a comfort.

They pushed onward through the perpetual twilight of the ancient forest. "I wish I knew where we were going exactly," Arthur said.

"Sometimes you have to keep going even if you don't know where it will get you," Morf told him.

"I suppose so."

And so they tramped on for what seemed like half a day, until gradually the forest began to thin out and they could make out individual trees. Patches of soft moss covered the forest floor. The path petered out and finally vanished beneath the moss.

Far ahead, the giant bees continued to signal, THIS WAY, THIS WAY.

"I hope they know what they're doing," said Arthur, who was tired and sore and hungrier than he'd ever been.

"I think we're almost there," Morf said. "Wherever *there* is."

There turned out to be a stand of immensely tall

trees. Trees as big as California redwoods, and probably much, much older. Hundreds of giant bees hovered around the base of the enormous trees, dancing elaborate signals in the air. They became very excited as the two visitors approached, but somehow Arthur sensed they weren't going to attack. Indeed, they seemed to be eagerly awaiting their arrival.

It wasn't until he was almost at the base of the tallest tree that Arthur saw the object that had so excited the bees. In a place where several of the trees grew together, roots entwined, the bees had constructed a remarkable hive. The hive looked as if it had been made of thick papier-mâché, and it was as big as a good-sized house.

Bees flew in and out via a series of entrances and exits that looked like stubby chimneys. Now the bees danced and swirled above and around the hive, spelling out a signal that Morf translated as, "WELCOME VISITORS, OUR HIVE IS YOUR HIVE."

"It's a very nice hive," Arthur said, trying to be polite. "But I hope they don't want us to live there."

The buzzing insects swirled into a formation for another signal.

"OUR HONEY IS YOUR HONEY," Morf translated. He added, "I think they're inviting us to eat."

A squadron of bees tore at the side of the hive, creating what at first appeared to be a window into their house. Almost immediately the air filled with a rich, sweet scent, and Arthur found himself drawn to the window as if by invisible strings.

Already the rich, amber-colored honey was beginning to ooze from the opening. The bees kept a respectful distance, but their incessant buzzing urged him to eat.

EAT AND BE STRONG, the bees signaled.

Arthur was so hungry, he'd actually been considering eating moss from the forest floor, so he didn't need a second invitation to try the honey. He scooped out a glob and licked it from his finger. Almost immediately his whole body trembled with relief. The honey was more than delicious; it was rich in nutrients, vitamins, and the mysterious essence of flower blossoms.

"Not bad," said Morf, licking his paw. "Not bad at all."

But Arthur was too busy eating the honey to reply. He filled his hands with the sticky stuff, and he let it roll down his throat. The honey was cool and warm at the same time, and the taste of it reverberated from the top of his head to the tips of his toes. The honey made his blood sparkle with energy and his brain hum with intelligence. It gave him strength and revived his courage.

Strangely enough, although he ate handfuls of the stuff, the honey didn't make him feel bloated or full. It was as if the honey somehow entered directly into his body, into his muscles and blood and bones, without having to pass through his stomach.

Eventually he wasn't hungry anymore, and he carefully licked his hands clean.

"What a revolting mess," Morf was saying. "I've somehow got honey on my tail."

While Morf groomed himself, Arthur sat down on the mossy floor of the forest and looked up at the enormously tall trees. Their tops were so high, they could barely be seen. But among the faint blur of distant leaves was a patch of sunlight, and the sunlight beamed all the way down through the trees and leaves and branches and bathed Arthur with its warmth.

For the first time since he'd said good-bye to the Cloud People, Arthur felt real hope. The hope that if he kept trying he would somehow achieve his goal, and the bees and the trees and the sky would continue to exist.

I must succeed, Arthur said to himself quite fiercely. *Everyone is counting on me.*

Suddenly the ground began to shake violently. The tall trees swayed, a wind blew up, and the bees became even more excited.

"What's that?" Arthur exclaimed in alarm.

Morf stopped licking his honey-soaked tail and looked up. "Sounds like a giant waking up," he said with a shrug. "Either that, or the world is already ending."

26

...

THE AWAKENING

WHEN THE TREES BEGAN to uproot themselves and crash to the ground, Arthur and Morf had no choice but to flee the forest. As they ran, more and more of the trees toppled over. The wind increased in velocity, stinging Arthur's eyes with bits of fine dirt.

"It's an earthquake!" he exclaimed.

"Can't be an earthquake," Morf corrected. "We're not on Earth, remember?"

Just then the ground shifted under their feet, and Arthur fell to his knees. Something huge was happening to the landscape. Directly in front of them, hills were rising, as if something deep below was forcing its way up to the surface.

Astonished, Arthur blinked dirt from his eyes as the

hills lifted higher and higher, shedding trees and clumps of moss.

And then, incredibly, the hills stood up.

"I might have known," Morf said, clinging to a patch of moss. For some reason he didn't seem particularly surprised.

Arthur stared as the hills shook themselves free of the dirt and rocks that had covered them for a thousand years. In the back of his mind he knew what was happening, but he still couldn't believe it.

When the dust settled, a giant stood swaying in the daylight. Bits of trees and vegetation still clung to the giant, who seemed to be in a terrible mood. Creaking like a mighty ship caught in a bad storm, the giant bent down, grasped its enormous foot, and howled in pain.

"ARGHHHHHHHHHHH! HURRRRRRRRRT!"

The cry of pain caused several small tornadoes to spin away, sucking up dirt and spewing it out like maddened vacuum cleaners. A squadron of bees had been stinging the giant's big toe, and they flew off quickly, before the giant could smash them with her angry fists.

Her fists. For Arthur saw that it was a female giant, with an enormous tangle of unkempt, dirt-clotted hair swinging down to her waist.

"HURRRRRRRRRRRRT!" the giant wailed, and her cry made bolts of lightning sizzle from cloud to cloud. Tears of pain fell from her eyes and washed through the gullies like small, ferocious floods.

The angry giant looked around for something to smash. The bees had fled to a safe distance, so her eyes alighted on two very small creatures close to hand.

With a roar she snatched up the ground where Arthur and Morf cowered.

"YOU HURT ME!" she bellowed, and she was about to close her mighty fist and crush them, when Arthur scrambled up on her thumb and shouted at the top of his lungs.

"Droll!" he cried. "Stop!"

Puzzled by the tiny voice, she hesitated. "DROLL?" She said it as if the word was unfamiliar. "WHO DROLL?"

"You are Droll!" Arthur shouted. "You must be! You and Grog are the last of the giants!"

"GROG? WHO GROG?"

Her fist partially closed, as if she were losing patience.

"Grog is the one who loves you!" Arthur cried, cupping his hands together to make his voice carry.

"GROG? LOVE?" The giant's voice softened a little, and the lightning stopped flashing from cloud to cloud. "CAN'T REMEMBER."

But the giant was curious enough to place Arthur and Morf on her shoulder, so their tiny words would be closer to her ear.

"You've been sleeping for a long, long time!" Arthur cried, knowing he was shouting for his very life. "Maybe a thousand years or more! But once upon a time you loved Grog and went to pick flowers for your wedding! You never returned! Grog still misses you!"

"GROG," the giant muttered, causing bits of trees and branches to unravel from her tangled hair. She struggled to remember, for she hadn't had time to fully awaken. "LOVE GROG? YES!" she thundered. "YES! YES! *YES!*"

"She remembers!" Arthur cried to Morf.

As Droll's memory slowly returned, she recalled what had happened on that day long ago. She had gone far afield to gather flowers for her wedding celebration. Since everyone on the planet was invited, she needed a great many flowers, and her search took her farther and farther, until she came to the end of the world.

"A DEEP, DARK PLACE," she said mournfully, as if the memory itself was painful. "THE CRACK IN THE BOTTOM OF THE WORLD. THE LAST FLOWER WAS THERE, GROWING FAR BELOW. IT WAS THE MOST BEAUTIFUL FLOWER OF ALL, AND I REACHED DOWN TO PICK IT."

And that's when the ground had split apart. The next thing she knew, she was falling. Droll fell for miles and miles, spinning and spinning. When at last she crashed into the place known as Beyond, rivers all over the world reversed direction. Tidal waves swept the planet, and the storm of Grog's sorrow did not abate for a hundred years.

Meanwhile, Droll slept the sleep of fallen giants. Moss grew over her, and then plants and trees, and finally a mighty forest, and still, she slept. She didn't wake until the bees uncovered her big toe and stung it again and again.

"The bees must have had a reason," Arthur told her. "They wouldn't have stung you if it wasn't important that you wake up."

"WHAT REASON?" the giant asked fearfully. "IS GROG DEAD?"

"No," Arthur told her. "He still waits for you by the sea. But he's given up hope that you'll ever return."

"I MUST GO TO HIM."

"Yes, of course," said Arthur. "But first you must help me."

Arthur told her about his journey and why he had to find the one called Vydel.

"VYDEL! VYDEL IS THE ONE WHO MADE ME SEE THE FLOWER," she said, her enormous eyes flashing with anger. "HE MADE ME FALL. HE WANTED THE LAST OF THE GIANTS TO DIE SO THAT HE COULD BE THE MOST POWERFUL OF ALL."

"If I don't find him, the last of the giants really might die, and so will Vydel, and everything else that lives."

Droll sighed, and a cool wind brought autumn to the world.

"I WILL TAKE YOU TO HIM," she said.

27

...

THE ISLAND
OF THE DEMON

DROLL'S CLOTHING WAS ragged after being buried for centuries, and her pockets had long ago disintegrated. So she placed Arthur and Morf in her tangled hair, and there they rode, swinging on rope-thick strands just below her left ear.

"Are you okay?" Arthur asked Morf, who didn't look at all well.

"I'll survive."

Droll was striding with a purpose, leaving behind the lush gardens and forests of the Beyond. She hurried through valleys, her great feet leaving impressions that would become ponds and lakes. She clambered over steep mountains and, in her haste, she ripped away parts of the horizon. And all the while, she grumbled and complained to herself.

"DROLL HATES THE DEMON. THE DEMON HATES DROLL. NO GOOD CAN COME OF THIS. SAY GOOD-BYE TO THE EVERYTHING." She muttered on and on until it finally dawned on Arthur that Droll was talking to herself because she was afraid.

If a creature as strong and powerful as a giant feared Vydel, was there any hope for a boy? And yet however much he feared facing the demon, the Nothing was infinitely worse.

After a while they came to a great plain that stretched as far as the eye could see. The ground was so far below that Arthur couldn't be sure, but the plain seemed to be covered with a kind of thin, yellow grass. There was nothing else—no trees, no hills, not even a rock to disturb the forever flatness of the land.

With no obstructions to climb over or around, Droll picked up her pace, stretching out her long legs mile after mile. Slowly the thin, yellow grass of the plains gave way to bare ground, and Arthur understood that they had entered a barren area where nothing lived, not even a blade of grass.

"What is this place?" he asked.

"We're in the middle of Nowhere," said Morf. "I've never been here before, but I recognize it from the descriptions."

Droll thundered along through Nowhere, and even her massive feet made no impression on the featureless landscape.

"MUST NOT GIVE UP," she muttered to herself. "MUST KEEP GOING."

Her stride never faltered. She kept on, churning across the miles, until at last Arthur glimpsed something at the edge of the world. At first it looked like a blob of light, melting along the horizon. Then he saw that it was a reflection of something shiny, and he understood that he was seeing water again.

After an hour or so they came to the edge, and Droll hesitated. Flat, colorless water stretched away in every direction. There were no waves, no currents, not even a ripple to disturb the everywhere sameness. It was like a liquid version of Nowhere.

"There's only one place this could be," said Morf. His voice was unusually solemn. "The Sea of the Dead."

Droll worked up her courage and dipped her sore, bee-stung toe in the water. She sighed deeply, creating a cloud that quickly dissipated, and then began to make her way into the Sea of the Dead. At first, it was no more than puddle-deep to Droll.

"GIANTS CAN'T SWIM," she announced, but it didn't seem to matter, because the water was barely up to her ankles. Soon enough, however, the water began to deepen until Droll could no longer lift her feet free and had to slog through it, knee-deep.

Then waist-deep.

Then up to her armpits—Ugh! Arthur didn't want to think about a giant's armpits. Then higher, up to her neck, until Arthur and Morf could feel the water lapping at their own feet, just inches below.

Meanwhile Droll gasped and burbled and kept on going. The water was up to her mouth, so she had to breathe through her nose. It sounded like a two-piston steam engine with a slow leak.

"If the water gets any deeper, we'll have to swim," said Arthur, clinging to the giant's dampening hair.

"You can't swim, remember?" said Morf. "Besides, nothing floats in the Sea of the Dead."

At the last possible moment, Droll's hand plucked them from her hair. She held them aloft as her great head submerged beneath the dull and colorless water. Bubbles burst from her mouth and nose, creating a froth that quickly disappeared, as if there were something about the Sea of the Dead that would not tolerate a disturbance.

Droll kept on going even though she could not breathe, for a giant's lungs are very large. But even a giant can drown if submerged for long enough, and Arthur was just about to beg her to turn around and go back—they'd have to find another way—when he saw an island sticking up from the flat and featureless sea.

The strange island looked like a black thorn poking through a dull plate of glass, for if the Sea of the Dead did not float, neither did it reflect. As is often the case, most of the island was actually submerged beneath the water; Droll sped to it and immediately began to scale the side of the island.

When her head came out of the water, she drew a deep breath that dropped barometric pressures a thousand miles away.

Then things began to happen very quickly. Before they were ready for it, Arthur and Morf found themselves deposited on the edge of the demon's island.

"DROLL WAITS FOR YOU," she announced, and she lolled in the shallow waters surrounding the island, having her first real bath in ten centuries.

"I guess we're here," Arthur said uncertainly.

"Hmmmm," said Morf. "We're on an island in the middle of a dead sea that's in the middle of nowhere at all. So, yeah, I guess we must be here."

"You needn't be so sarcastic."

"Sorry, kid," said Morf. "I sometimes get sarcastic when I'm scared to death."

Yet Morf, as usual, didn't look the least bit frightened, which made Arthur feel slightly less nervous. The island was made of a dull, glassy-looking substance, and nothing grew upon it.

"I'll bet this whole island came out of a volcano somehow," said Arthur. They explored just beyond the water's edge.

"That's because it *is* a volcano," Morf told him.

"Which makes sense, because volcanoes are destructive but beautiful, and that's how demons think of themselves."

The above-water part of the island was actually quite small. They found they could walk all the way around it in about ten minutes. But what the island lacked in circumference, it made up in height. The sharp, thorn-shaped peak loomed far above them, as if attempting to pierce the pale green sky.

"Well," said Arthur, "Vydel isn't down here, so he must be up there."

"Must be, I suppose."

"We've come all this way to ask him a question," said Arthur. "We can't quit now."

"Why not?"

"Because it will be the end of Everything."

"So?" Morf said it ever so casually. "Everything has to end sometime, right?"

"Maybe. But it's not going to end right now just because I didn't try hard enough."

Morf smiled. "I was testing your resolve, Arthur— lack of confidence is fatal when confronting demons—and you passed the test with flying colors. Lead on, Arthur Courage." Morf bowed from the waist. "Lead, and I will follow. To the end of the world and the land Beyond. To the middle of Nowhere and the Sea of the Dead. To the Island of the Demon, and the demon himself—lead on!"

28

. . .

THE THING
INSIDE THE BOX

IT TOOK ALL OF Arthur's strength to make the climb. The sides of the peak were smooth and slippery, and he had to cling with his hands and his feet, inching himself upward.

Maddeningly, Morf seemed to keep up without having to exert himself.

"Only a demon would live in a stupid place like this," Arthur said, grunting with effort.

"I'm sure you're right."

At last they came to a narrow ledge, although it was nearly as slippery as the sloping sides of the peak. Arthur heaved himself over the edge and sat there panting as he caught his breath. Morf, naturally, looked as rested as if he'd been lounging in a chair at the beach.

"There'd be a nice view from here," he commented, "if only there was something to see."

"Where's that crummy demon?" asked Arthur, for he was very frustrated. "I'll bet he's hiding just to make it difficult for us."

"No doubt," said Morf. "Unless he lives in that box."

"Box?" said Arthur. "What box?"

On the inside corner of the ledge was a box made of some sort of black metal. Or maybe it was carved from colorless stone—it was hard to tell. The box, which was about the size of a small television set, had been built into the slope of the upper peak. Instead of a screen, the box had a solid-looking door, and the door was fastened shut with a big, ancient padlock.

Affixed to the lock was a small paper tag.

THERE IS NO KEY, it said on the paper tag. FIND A WAY TO OPEN ME OR DIE TRYING.

The note was signed, VYDEL.

"Of all the rotten luck," Arthur fumed. "We came all this way, and now there's no way to open the lock!"

Arthur sat down, completely discouraged. But he leaped up right away because the surface of the ledge was hot. Hot and getting hotter.

Morf was already dancing around on his little feet.

"You'd better hurry!" he cried. "In about three minutes we'll be frying like eggs!"

It was obvious that if they didn't find a way to open the padlock, they would indeed die trying, as the note had promised. Arthur's shoes began to steam, and his feet were hotter than they'd ever been, hotter even than the day he'd made the mistake of trying to cross the beach without his sandals. *Much* hotter.

"It's no use!" he cried. "We can't get back down the way we came, because everything is burning!"

Morf's little feet were sizzling like sausages in a pan, but instead of complaining, he said, "You must have an idea! You must!"

But Arthur's only idea was that his friend should escape while he still had the chance. "Change, Morf! Change!"

Arthur expected Morf to change into a bird and fly away. Instead, he was astonished to see the little creature morph himself into a long, slender garden snake. Before Arthur had a chance to be afraid—and he was terribly frightened of snakes of all kinds—Morf slithered across the hottest part of the ledge, heading right for the box.

When he got to the box, the Morf-snake slipped into the keyhole in the ancient padlock. He writhed and squirmed and pushed, and a moment later the hasp popped free, and the lock opened.

Instantly the ledge was cool again.

"An excellent idea you had," Morf said when he was himself again.

Arthur was about to protest that it wasn't his idea, not really, when slowly the door to the box opened wide.

"Who opened me?" said a small, reedy voice.

The box appeared to be empty, but clearly it was not. At least not in the usual sense of the word.

"WHO OPENED ME?" it demanded, louder this time.

"Us," Arthur confessed. "Or rather, me."

"Which is it?" said the voice in a nasty tone.

Arthur didn't want to get Morf in trouble, and, anyhow, it was his journey, so he said, "It was me."

"There are billions of me's," said the voice inside the box. "Which me are you, specifically?"

"I'm Arthur," said Arthur, and he started to add "Woodbury," until he thought better of it. "Arthur, um, Arthur Courage."

"Hmpf!" said the voice. "A preposterous name for a fat little boy. Are you sure?"

"Yes," said Arthur. "I'm sure."

"You are allowed one question," said the box. "If it's the right question, you get an answer. If it's the wrong question, you die."

. . .

And so, at last, the time had come.

Arthur took a deep breath. He tried to steady his

quaking knees. He said, "My question is this: How do I get home?"

The box was silent for a moment. And then it began to laugh. It was not a friendly kind of laugh, either. It was a laugh of triumphant cruelty. "What a stupid question! And obviously the wrong question, too. Why should I tell you, a mere boy, how to get home?"

Suddenly the ledge was hot again, much hotter than before.

"Because if you don't tell me, you die, too!" said Arthur, dancing from foot to foot as his shoes smoldered.

"Ridiculous!" roared the empty box. "Nothing can kill me!"

"Exactly!" Arthur shouted. "The Nothing *can* kill you! And if I don't find my way home and stop the Nothing, Everything will cease to exist, and that includes *you*!"

Just as suddenly as it had heated up, the ledge under his smoldering feet cooled down. Not all the way, but enough so his shoes weren't burning.

"Explain," said the box. "And this better be good or I'll turn you into a bacon crisp and fry your soul for dessert."

Arthur told the box how his Other Self was still on Earth, fast asleep, which meant he was in two places at once, which was clearly impossible, which meant the Nothing had somehow found a crack and leaked into the universe. Which in turn meant that if he didn't find a way to stop it, it would be the end of Everything.

"And why should I believe you?" said the box.

"Because you know Everything," Arthur said. "Or that's the rumor, anyway. And if you know Everything, then it stands to reason that you must know about the Nothing, too. Therefore you know that what I've told you is true, even if it seems impossible."

The box was silent. And then a shadow moved inside the box, and a head became visible.

A human head. A head that was strangely familiar to Arthur.

The head smiled. It was a kind and gentle face, and immediately Arthur felt an intense longing, for this was a face he had wanted to see for the whole of his short life.

"Don't you recognize me?" asked the head inside the box.

"I-I'm not sure," Arthur stammered.

"Don't be afraid. Speak from your heart."

Arthur felt like weeping, but he managed to keep the tears from falling by tipping up his face. "I've only seen him in photo albums, and in the silly video my mom plays when she's feeling sad, but you look exactly like my father."

"And have you always wanted to see me?" the head asked. "More than anything? Have you wanted to see me more than you wanted to be thin? More than you wanted to have friends?"

"Yes," Arthur said, letting his tears fall at last. "Oh yes, more than anything."

The head began to laugh uproariously, and it was no longer his father's kindly head but the head of a small, ugly demon. A demon with eyes like chips of ice and teeth as sharp as needles. "Fool!" the demon roared. "Like all humans, you only want what you can never have!"

Arthur sniffed and dried his eyes. "So? What's wrong with that?"

"Everything!" Vydel screamed. "Everything and Nothing!"

Arthur wiped his eyes. He was angry at himself for letting the demon trick him. "You haven't answered my question," he said stubbornly. "How do I get home?"

"Fool!" the demon screeched. "Humans are so stupid! They ask a question when they already know the answer. You want to know how to get home? Use your imagination!"

"What?" asked Arthur.

"You heard me. USE YOUR IMAGINATION!"

And with that, the door to the demon box slapped shut, and the ancient padlock relocked itself.

29

...

A WONDER
AND A TERROR
TO BEHOLD

THEY HAD BEEN all the way to the end of the world and beyond, and what good had it done them?

Stupid demon.

For the duration of their long journey back, Arthur sulked and fidgeted. He was barely aware of the changing landscape that passed beneath Droll's thundering feet. What occupied his thoughts was how the demon had tormented him with a brief glimpse of his father's face and then snatched it cruelly away.

Until that moment, Arthur hadn't understood how much he'd missed having a father, and now that he did understand, he wished he hadn't. As Vydel had said, what was the point of wanting something you could never have?

Oh, that was bad enough, but even worse was the demon's answer: *"Use your imagination."* Talk about lame advice! That's what stupid teachers said when they handed you blank sheets of paper. That's what stupid mothers said when you complained about being bored.

Stupid, stupid, stupid.

He'd been the stupidest one of all, thinking that a rotten demon who lived in a box would help him save the universe.

"Penny for your thoughts," Morf said as Droll lumbered down from the high mountains, into the valleys behind the Beyond.

"Keep your penny," Arthur said bitterly. "It's pointless."

"What's pointless?"

"Everything. I'll never get back home. I'll never be thin. I'll never see my father. I'll never stop the Nothing, and soon we'll all disappear, and there will never be anybody to know we existed!"

Morf sighed. "That bad, is it?"

"Worse!" said Arthur vehemently.

"You sound as if you've given up."

Arthur felt like lashing out at someone, and as it wasn't wise to lash out at a giant, the only one available was Morf. And so he turned on Morf with a sneer. "What did you expect from a boy everyone calls

Biscuit Butt, huh? You expect a boy like that to actually do anything? What a complete waste of time!"

"Complete waste of time, huh? Would you care to define that?"

"The Frog People, the boat, the big wave, the windstorm, the giant, the Cloud People, the stupid borons, Mr. Pockets, the River Beneath the World, the raft, the river serpents, the bees, the other giant, going to see the rotten demon," he said, ticking off everything he'd seen or done in REM World. "ALL OF IT! A COMPLETE WASTE OF TIME!"

"Oh, really?" Morf said archly. "You missed 'learning to fly.' Was that a complete waste of time, too?"

For some reason the mention of learning to fly really made Arthur seethe. "It was fun while it lasted, but so what? What good did it do me? What good did it do anyone?"

"Some things can't be measured that way," said Morf. "Arthur Courage knew that."

Which made Arthur feel like the top of his head was going to blow off. "Arthur Courage is dead!" he shouted. "He's so dead, he never existed!"

Morf looked as if he wanted to say something, but then he changed his mind. He remained silent for the rest of the journey.

· · ·

Droll never slowed her pace, so anxious was she to get back to the world, and to Grog. With her two tiny passengers safe in the tangle of her hair, she slogged her way out of the Sea of the Dead. She crossed through the barren plains of Nowhere, and followed her own footprints back into the Beyond. From there she climbed out of the World Below and, smelling the scent of a planet teeming with life—and with Grog—she ran for the horizon, causing fractures so large in the tectonic plates of REM World that new continents formed and old continents slowly vanished beneath the waves.

Giants in love can be dangerous beings, a wonder and a terror to behold. Half a world away, Grog woke up to the sound of Droll's heart beating, and his joy was such that he ran like a hurricane. The wind of him flattened forests, blew rivers from their banks, and turned ten of the Eleven Seas to foam.

Droll, being somewhat more sensible, stopped running when she heard Grog coming, and waited. Which was a wise thing to do, since two giants colliding at full speed are likely to set off a spontaneous nuclear explosion and blow themselves into atoms and quarks and other particles so small, they are the exact opposite of giants.

"TAKE COVER," Droll advised, setting her little passengers down while she awaited the arrival of Grog.

Arthur and Morf found themselves on a beach—quite a familiar beach, actually, although they didn't have time to notice that before Grog himself loomed over the horizon.

"DROLL LIVES!" he roared, in a voice that flattened the hurricanes trailing in his wake. "DROLL LIVES, AND I AM HAPPY AGAIN!"

The two lonely giants embraced, shedding a thousand years of sorrow and creating enough static electricity to power thunderstorms for eight or nine millennia, give or take. But there would be no rain on this day, for the heat of their joy brought a bright summer warmth to REM World, and the green sky was clear and beautiful.

Droll and Grog vowed to get married as soon as their guests arrived, which would take a while, since every living creature would once again be invited to their wedding.

Meanwhile Arthur wandered along the strangely familiar beach, kicking at clumps of seaweed. It seemed so cruel—just as Grog and Droll found each other, the universe was about to end.

"Pointless," he muttered to himself. "Everything is so pointless. We're born, we live, we die—what does it matter what happens in between? It doesn't last. Nothing lasts, not even the universe!"

Morf followed behind him, kicking at the same piles of seaweed. The fog was rolling in, and this, too, was strangely familiar.

"Maybe you've got it all wrong," Morf suggested. "Maybe the Nothing was always there, and because it's nothing, it can't do us any harm."

Arthur sighed. "Have a look for yourself," he said to his friend, holding out the wristwatch. "It's hopeless."

Morf looked into the dark face of the watch. The terrible, dark Nothing had risen up to the level of the workbench in Arthur's basement, and soon it would cover the boy's sleeping face.

There was no doubt that the Nothing was eating away everything and leaving nothing behind, because the darkness it made wasn't merely dark. Not the dark of shadows, or of night, nor even the dark of fear itself. The dark of the Nothing was emptiness, and absence of everything that had ever lived or existed, and absence even of the dead and those who remembered them. In the Nothing, stars had never shined, flowers had never bloomed, children had never laughed, love had never existed.

The Nothing was nothing, just nothing at all, forever and ever.

"I must admit it does look grim," Morf said, turning away from the watch. "It hardly seems worth doing anything, if we're all about to vanish. Still, the fog is beautiful today, don't you agree?"

"Fog?" asked Arthur.

He'd had his head down and hadn't noticed the fog rolling in. It was beautiful, in an eerie sort of way. It reminded Arthur of things he'd forgotten to remember. For instance, the strong smell of the seaweed when he'd first arrived on REM World, which was exactly how the seaweed smelled right now. And maybe because of that, he wasn't at all surprised to see shapes approaching through the fog, shapes that had once frightened him but that now he recognized as Frog People.

The first to emerge from the fog was Galump. She smiled at Arthur in her kindly way, and his heart broke as he ran to her. "I'm so sorry," he sobbed, embracing her. "I failed, Galump. I failed."

Galump hugged him so hard he could feel her heart beating. "You can't have failed," she said. "You're Arthur Courage, and you earned that name. Courage is not about success or failure."

"But the Nothing is going to win," he sobbed. "I tried to get home and stop it, but I can't."

Galump took him by the shoulders and stood him up. She dried his eyes with a small kerchief made of sea silk. "You must *keep* trying, Arthur. Even when there seems to be no hope. That's the only way to keep the Nothing from winning."

Arthur took a deep breath and got control of himself. "You've been very kind, all of you, and for a while you made me feel like a real hero. But the truth is, I'm just a fat, lonely boy without any real friends, or a father to show me how to do things, and I'm just not smart enough or brave enough to save the whole universe."

Galump considered this. "There are three things

you should know, Arthur Courage. The first is that although your father is dead, part of him survives in you, and helps make you who you are. The second thing is that you are exactly brave enough and exactly smart enough to save the universe, or else you wouldn't have been chosen for the task. The third thing is that to accomplish your goal, you must use what you learned from the demon in the box."

"But—"

"No buts. And no biscuits, either. Those days are behind you." Galump coughed. "Hear me, Arthur Courage. The demon in the box was not always a demon. Once, long ago, he was on the side of all that was good, and he used his powers wisely. Since time grows short, I will not go into all the details of his story, which could fill a book, or several books. Let us simply say that the lust for more and more power was Vydel's downfall, and now he is doomed to live in a trap of his own devising. You know him as a thing of evil, and that he certainly is, but the angel within still exists, and that part makes him speak the truth. Whatever he told you about how to find your way home, that is the truth, the whole truth, and nothing but the truth."

"But all he said was, 'Use your imagination.'"

"And so you must," Galump told him. "It is the only way home, from where you are now."

"But I don't understand!"

Galump reached out and stroked his hair. "Everything you need is right here," she said, tapping his forehead. "Go with our love, dear boy, but go you must."

And with that, Galump and the other Frog People returned into the mist and fog, and when Arthur looked for him, Morf was gone, too. All he heard, fading away into the fog, was a faint, faint voice calling out, "You can do it, kid!" and then the voice, too, vanished utterly, leaving only empty silence behind.

Arthur was alone. As alone as he had ever been. So alone that he ached from the inside out, which made him want to go home more than ever, wherever home was, and whatever awaited him there.

"*Use your imagination,*" the thing in the box had said.

And so he did.

3 0

. . .

THE END OF
THE BEGINNING

SURROUNDED BY THE soft white fog, Arthur closed
his eyes and tried to imagine his way home. In his
mind he pictured the house where he'd grown up,
and all the windows that looked out onto the world,
and all the rooms inside the house.

He imagined the furniture in each of the rooms, and
the paintings on the walls, and the posters in his bed-
room. He imagined the model planes he'd never finished,
and the books he hadn't read, and the little desk where
he'd found so many reasons not to do his homework.

He imagined the warm smells of his mother's cook-
ing, and the funny way his grandmother laughed
when she was happy, and the different way she

laughed when she was mad. He imagined the cool, crisp feel of the floor under his feet, and the way the carpets made his bare toes tickle.

He imagined all of the memories that home had given him, the good ones and the bad. He imagined the taste of cookies and milk, and the lovely cake he'd had for his birthday, and for all the birthdays as far back as he could remember. He imagined riding down the banister when they told him not to, and the time he sprained his ankle, and the tears he'd shed when the other children called him names. He imagined being happy and sad and everything in between.

He imagined the basement, his secret, private place, and the mysterious tools that had once belonged to his father, and would someday be his, if only he learned how to use them. He imagined himself on the workbench, and the steps that led up to the bulkhead, and the way the sky looked when he threw open the door. A sky so blue, and so perfect, it made you glad to be alive.

When he'd built the house in his mind, and filled it with all the things he knew, he opened his eyes.

And there in the fog, looking so real and solid he could almost reach out and touch it, was the bulkhead door.

Go on, he told himself, *what have you got to lose?*

So Arthur reached for the handle and lifted the door. Just below the door were the old, familiar wooden steps that led down into the basement.

He was halfway down the steps before he saw the

Nothing. There was no longer any floor to the basement, and the Nothing was rising fast, eating up the walls. From where he stood he could just make out the corner of the workbench where his Other Self lay fast asleep, unaware that Everything was about to end.

"Wake up, you doofus!" he shouted. "Hey, lamebrain, wake up!"

But his Other Self lay unmoving, his face and ears covered by the special helmet.

Arthur was so close, but how could he get from here to there?

The Nothing slowly rose higher, eating the step just below his feet. He had to do something, and right this instant.

Arthur looked up, and his eyes lighted on the plumbing pipes that ran through the floor joists.

Without thinking about it, or what would happen if he missed, he jumped up and grabbed a pipe.

He swung away from the steps, and now there was no going back. So he reached and grabbed the next pipe, swinging himself forward. Arthur reached for the next pipe, and the next, and before he knew it, he was directly over the workbench, directly above his Other Self.

"Wake up," he begged himself. "Wake up!"

And then his hands slipped, and he fell on top of his Other Self, and everything went black.

. . .

Arthur couldn't see a thing. Everything was dark. Darker than night, darker than dreams, exactly as dark as the Nothing. This, surely, was the end.

Blindly he brought his hands up to his eyes—and that's when he felt the helmet on his head.

Instantly he sat up and pushed away the helmet and was dazed by the single lightbulb hanging above the workbench.

Out of the corner of his eye he saw the terrible, dark Nothing vanishing down into the farthest corners of the basement. But when he tried to look directly at it, it was gone, and the basement and his house was exactly as it had always been.

With a mixture of fear and pure joy he leaped down from the workbench and rushed up the basement stairs to the kitchen.

"Hello!" he cried, opening the door. "Is anybody home?"

His mother turned from the refrigerator, where she'd been putting the party food away.

"Of course we're here. Where would we go?"

Arthur rushed up to his mother and gave her a hug, which was very unlike him. "I'm so glad to be home," he said. "So totally, totally glad."

"Glad to be home?" she said, sounding concerned. "Where have you been?"

"I've had the most terrible dream," he said. "And the most wonderful dream, too. I can't really explain it. But I really am glad to be home, even if I never went anywhere at all, even if it was all a dream."

"What a strange boy you are!" His mother looked puzzled, but she was smiling.

That's when Arthur remembered to feel in his pockets for the cookies he'd taken down into the basement.

The cookies were gone.

"Why, look at you!" his mother said, staring at him, amazed. "I hadn't noticed before. You're not fat anymore. You're thin! As thin as your father when he was your age!"

Arthur looked. It was true. He'd gone down into the basement fat, and he'd come back thin. Gloriously, triumphantly thin. Well, not thin exactly, but not fat, either. Certainly not fat.

"It worked," he said, and his eyes were big and full of surprise. "It really worked!"

"What worked, dear?" his mother asked.

"Everything. I learned to do stuff like pull-ups, and row a boat, and fly, and ride the giants, and save the universe."

"What?" his mother asked, as if she hadn't heard him clearly. "What did you say?"

"Oh, nothing," said Arthur.

And he went out into the world, the real world, his own world, and he knew in his heart that he wasn't Biscuit Butt, or Goodyear the human blimp. From this day on, he had a new name, one he'd earned for himself.

Arthur Courage.

About this Scholastic Signature Author

RODMAN PHILBRICK is an award-winning author of books for both adults and young readers. Writing since the age of sixteen, he has published more than a dozen novels and numerous short stories, articles, and reviews. His first novel for young readers, *Freak the Mighty*, published by the Blue Sky Press in 1993, was named an ALA Best Book for Young Adults, a Judy Lopez Memorial Award Honor Book, and an ALA Quick Pick. *Freak the Mighty* was made into the 1998 Miramax feature film *The Mighty*. Philbrick's sequel, *Max the Mighty*, received starred reviews, and his novel *The Fire Pony* received the 1996 Capital Choice Award. His most recent book for the Blue Sky Press is *The Last Book in the Universe*. Mr. Philbrick and his wife, also a writer, divide their time between homes in Maine and the Florida Keys.